In his previous life, Peter Williams travelled widely with the RAF for twenty-two years, during which time he saw active service in what used to be the British Cameroon and Borneo.

He lives in relatively quiet retirement in Cornwall with his wife, spending much of his free time on the golf course.

He has previously written a compendium of short stories, *Words on Words*, and a book on the origins of religion, *Religion as Myth*.

Works in progress comprise a sequel to Aurora – Evolution?; a detective novel; numerous short stories; and his biography.

AURORA-EVOLUTION?

Peter Williams

A U R O R A - E V O L U T I O N ?

Vanguard Press

VANGUARD PAPERBACK

© Copyright 2009
Peter Williams

The right of Peter Williams to be identified as author of
this work has been asserted by him in accordance with the
Copyright, Designs and Patents Act 1988.

All Rights Reserved

No reproduction, copy or transmission of this publication
may be made without written permission.
No paragraph of this publication may be reproduced,
copied or transmitted save with the written permission of the publisher,
or in accordance with the provisions
of the Copyright Act 1956 (as amended).

Any person who commits any unauthorised act in relation to
this publication may be liable to criminal
prosecution and civil claims for damages.

A CIP catalogue record for this title is
available from the British Library.

ISBN 978 1 84386 568 1

Vanguard Press is an imprint of
Pegasus Elliot MacKenzie Publishers Ltd.
www.pegasuspublishers.com

First Published in 2009

Vanguard Press
Sheraton House Castle Park
Cambridge England

Printed & Bound in Great Britain

Foreword

As will become clear as you proceed with your reading of this book, the original Charles Darwin-Quirke was an inveterate recorder of his life's experiences and discoveries. Since his death, all his successors, being my creations, have been allowed to develop that same trait, and it is their continuing story that I present to you now, before the community referred to throughout as 'Aurora', of which I am an integral part, begin our departure from this Universe.

Upon the death of my friend and mentor, the original Charles Darwin-Quirke, I published his memoirs. It became a truly universal best seller, and the proceeds of that success made his descendants very rich indeed. When his line died out, the continuing royalties reverted to me via devious routes, and I have used them to assist in the furthering of my own evolution. You will no doubt be aware that many millions of years have elapsed since the original Charles Darwin-Quirke lived, and he and his 'Book of Memories' have fallen out of history into the complex realm of human mythology.

The extracts included in this work come from the very few remaining copies of his original book still extant among the human worlds. Although I possess the original manuscript, I have decided that, under circumstances that will become evident as you read on, I will withhold it from Humankind.

Authority has relegated the man and the artefact he named 'Aurora' to the realm of mythology, and in so doing overlooked the fact that in all mythologies there exists a kernel of truth. As a co-contributor to that original work, I reproduce it here in part, as the introduction to the continuing story of Aurora, and as proof positive of the reality that preceded the myth.

Aurora, AI (registered identity)

Introduction

We cannot assume that the universe we inhabit was the result of an explosion emanating from a zero energy state. The entirety of modern science dictates the impossibility of that scenario, and this leads to the assumption that the 'Big Bang', that brought this universe into being, resulted from events unknowable at this time. However, it is certain that somewhere in the production of the matter that contains this universe – or earlier versions of it – zero must figure. It is unfortunate that the science of Humankind has not yet sufficiently advanced to make any positive determinations in this regard.

There are four forces currently acting on the matter that constitutes this universe, and the science of Quantum Mechanics posits the belief that (in all probability), there were in the order of thirteen forces relating to and acting upon the matter that immediately preceded the appearance of this reality. From the moment of the 'Big Bang', they were reduced to just four by the mechanics of the sciences to which they were subservient from that moment. These forces are: Electromagnetism, The Strong and Weak Nuclear effects, and Gravity.

Perhaps all the forces in operation immediately prior to the event that gave birth to this universe had begun to weaken, and that the relative collapse of Gravity – the weakest force – precipitated that event.

It is here, in whatever preceded the 'Big Bang', that Humankind today places the deity they constructed out of primeval ignorance, and which they claim supposedly created this universe and all that it contains.

Such a 'deity', residing in the alternate reality from which this universe sprang so violently, may have been nothing more than a 'Man', a scientist who set out to provide a new habitat for his species because the one in which he then lived was moving toward the end of its habitable period. His universe was dying, just as will the one in which we exist, in the fullness of time.

Once brought into existence by the collapsing of a black hole in that reality, resulting in the 'Big Bang' in this, this universe slowly stabilised, relatively speaking, by the deliberate reduction and restructuring of the restraining forces previously referred to, into those we recognise today. The mixture that eventually became our reality coalesced, equalised, and distributed itself throughout the rapidly expanding envelope that contained it. Thus it remained, until time decided the introduction of the harbinger of Life, Bacteria, into the biospheres of certain worlds in those galaxies considered suitable for the purpose, after which they evolved in whatever ways they would.

Approximately one-third of the distance through the life of this 'new' universe, and at the beginning of its habitable period, that universe from which this one spawned became barren, and began its final descent into entropy. The species it had previously nurtured finally realised the means by which the remnants of their race could leave on the long journey necessary to take up domicile in their engineered 'Garden in Eden' in this universe, on those planets therein considered capable of sustaining new life.

The journey from the instantaneous moment of their departure from that dead reality and their insertion into this took uncountable lifetimes, until the knowledge of their origins receded from history to exist only in mythology and racial memory.

And so it is today. Such suns as are able, support Life in all its great variety and humanity is once again at the apogee it enjoyed prior to its Diaspora from that first reality. Today, tribal memories, the mist and inaccessibility of time, continue to shroud and obscure them, bringing about a similar mythology. Even so, indomitable evolution is causing Humankind to strive to unravel what went before, back to and even before the origin of this universe, and to attempt to circumvent that which they now know will inevitably come again in this reality.

There have been many victories savoured and catastrophes lamented, yet still Humankind strives to create a continuing environment for Life out in the intractable vastness of this expanding universe. As he has before, so he will again succeed, and as before, so he will need the guidance of something or someone outside the realm of existing human experience...

Extract from 'The Book of Memories'.

by Charles Darwin-Quirke
(by courtesy of the Galactic Free Library)

Publishers Legally Required Disclaimer:

Edict, **No. 120098**, issued by the **Office of the Prelate of, and Advocate for, the Universal Church of the Creator**, which governs all such writings stipulated therein, states that:

'None of the conclusions arrived at or assumed by the author claiming to be Charles Darwin-Quirke in this extended extract of his supposed Memoirs regarding the origins of Humankind are provable by the application of current science, and are therefore to be considered a fiction, and as such consigned to the sphere of dubious mythology, along with the remaining contents of this work. The historically documented system of religious belief that generated the above referenced edict dictates that the whole book entitled 'Aurora – Evolution?' is apocryphal.

From this great distance, some three millennia on from the events Charles Darwin-Quirke and his imaginative construct claim to portray, it is impossible to accord the activity of the unknown entity misguided mythology calls 'Aurora' any discernable degree of accuracy.

There can be no place in this modern universe for the acceptance of vague mythology and altruistic falsities in lieu of the proven reality of the Universal Church and its espoused Religion.'

Prologue

Dream into Nightmare

It is over. Humankind's Great Dream is dead. All the thousands of years spent by men in yearning and dreaming of travelling between the stars, have been to no avail. A fine, great dream has turned into nightmare. The one hundred and fifty hard years of shipbuilding and preparation that were devoted to the species' first great Diaspora into the Milky Way galaxy are as nothing. As dust in the wind.

In the twentieth century, with primitive technology and even less knowledge, the minds of great men enabled Humankind to circle and view the Earth from outside the safety of her atmospheric envelope.

We hailed those early cosmonauts as heroes, yet their journeys were no more hazardous, bearing in mind the level of technology available, than those blind voyages undertaken by our seafaring ancestors in their frail wooden ships, with inaccurate instrumentation and debilitating diseases, during Mankind's exploration of the planet Earth in those far-off days. In fact, their exploits carried the risk of a greater range of dangers in the form of other, hostile life forms, and limitless angry and unpredictable oceans. Then, with the Industrial Age barely begun, but with greatly improved technology and knowledge, we journeyed to our natural satellite, the moon.

The cost of that and subsequent human-crewed expeditions was crippling to the national economies involved. Humankind reluctantly withdrew from further expeditions into space, restricting his activities to local excursions just outside the Earth's atmosphere, allowing the use of resultant financial savings for the attempted subjugation of foreign regimes, in order to rectify their perceived inadequacies. This often prolonged interference in the lives of others on the planet, albeit for professed altruistic reasons – although greed and envy were at the core of all such activity – only succeeded in delaying the realisation of Mankind's dream of space conquest, and limited the time spent in corrective introspection regarding the functioning of their own fallible and corrupt administrations.

After a lapse of many years, private but desultory Earth orbit satellite experimentation bore fruit, allowing the building of sumptuous palaces in geo-synchronous orbits for the traditional money and the Nuevo Riche to stage their millennia-old sport of upstaging the Jones'.

However, alongside this remunerative business, investigation into long-term space habitat and travel requirements resulted in many short-term excursions around the solar system. Visits to planets, asteroids, and comets – first by robotic drones and then by humans – took place in rapid succession. The Moon became an early target for the establishment of human habitats and mining camps. Those intrepid pioneers who made the transition from the privations experienced on Earth for life on the Moon simply exchanged one form of poverty for another.

The major world powers that embroiled themselves in the vision of the final space accolade being theirs, spent sparse national resources financing that aim, only to fail as their economies fell toward poverty and abject reliance upon the help of other nations.

Finally, market forces prevailed and the major corporations created a one-world oligarchy. They pooled planetary resources and laid contingency plans for a massive Diaspora to planets discovered circling other, alien suns. World Government considered this Diaspora essential because of Mankind's inability to control his excesses, or to maintain the Earth in a habitable condition. Therefore, World Government acquired the necessary materials by mining the Moon and the asteroid belt, devising technologies, and developing the expertise to build the ships that would allow humanity to seed the galaxy.

At the end of the twenty-first century, climate degradation, allied to population pressure and the inability of a dying Earth to support a population level of forty billions, an excessively high level with regard to the surface area of the planet then available, dictated that humanity would soon have to expand into other stellar systems, much as did our forbears into the unknown lands of Earth in our distant history.

Many dreamed of the whole galaxy being inhabited by Humankind, and grandiose schemes were promulgated to direct this explosion of Humankind into that which they considered to be their Created Heritage, their Right!

These plans were, for centuries, just plans, for propulsion systems of the day required that ships carry their own fuel loads, thereby seriously limiting both attainable speed and distance. They finally became reality with the invention of the Faster-than-Light Drive (FTLD), which was soon nicknamed the 'Quirky' drive after its Australian inventor, Darwin 'Quirky' Quirke. This revolutionary drive system – barely understood by most of its users even today – utilised single point energy as its fuel source, and brought interstellar travel times into the realm of human understanding and life span.

Decades passed in a flurry of intense construction at space docks located in geo-stationary orbits around the Earth and Moon until eventually, after much pomp and publicity, the first of the great ships was finished. Thirty kilometres in length, and five in diameter, she looked from the surface of the Earth like a sleek and slender needle, with an eight-kilometre diameter ball in place of the eye, reflecting the sunlight from her glass reinforced spun Tritendium metal hull.

It was rumoured that the ship, thanks to the unique material from which the hull was constructed, could survive a direct hit from an asteroid that would devastate the Earth. For anything larger that might be encountered en route, she was equipped with a nuclear arsenal of a size incalculable to the average man, and all controlled by an organically grown Artificial Intelligence buried deep within the heart of the ship, to shield its delicate circuitry from the killing ravages of the hard radiation that permeates the vacuum of space. Its eyes were optical sensors distributed liberally over the hull, and were effective throughout the light spectrum. The great ship's sub space and main faster than light engines were contained within in the eight-kilometre diameter sphere attached by three huge struts aft of the hull, and drew the energy required for their function from the very fabric of space itself.

Entrepreneurial opportunists made overnight fortunes selling replicas of the vessel and its Artificial Intelligence remote controlled maintenance units and personnel flivvers. Then, with a rush of activity, the colonists, all volunteers, were loaded into their Metabolic Suspension 'Hibernation-cells'. The AI brought the great engines on line, and the enormous star ship powered up her operating systems and slowly oriented herself toward her destination.

The Great Day finally arrived, and Mankind took the first small step of the longest journey ever before dreamed. The first FTLD vessel, The Earth Research Expeditionary Star Ship 'Aurora', accelerated smoothly out of Earth orbit and the sun's gravity well en route for distant Alpha Centauri with a full complement of one hundred and ten thousand sleeping colonists and crew. Mere months later she was followed by a great fleet of two thousand five hundred star class vessels targeted at other destinations, near and far, each conveying a further one hundred and ten thousand immigrants apiece together with their equipment and supplies, all volunteers demanding new beginnings on worlds less crowded and polluted than the dying planet of their birth.

Many of the voyagers carried within their DNA latent genes, state of the art additions, specifically designed to manifest themselves in the first generation of children born to the colonists. These would enable speedier assimilation into the environments they expected to experience on their designated planets. Others enjoyed increased lung capacity to enable their survival in low oxygen atmospheres, and still others had vastly increased strength and metabolic rates for those planets with higher than Earth gravity.

Without exception, their publicity releases claimed that they would respect their new homes in a way Humankind had failed to do here on Earth, by avoiding repeats of Earth's ecological and cultural disasters.

All appeared to be going well until the first ship of the Diaspora fleet, the ERESS Aurora, dropped into temporal space upon her approach to the Alpha Centauri System, and re-established communication with an eager and optimistic Earth. All readings were nominal, but the ship notified Diaspora control that it had been unable to awaken the duty crews from Hibernation – a form of cryogenic suspension – since the jump to light speed, and that they and the one hundred and ten thousand hibernating colonists were devoid of all signs of life. The ship's AI was unable to determine the reason for this apparent anomaly.

One hundred and ten thousand souls, plus crew, dead in the cold of space... How was it that such an eventuality was allowed to go unsuspected?

Over time, this question recurred repeatedly, as one by one the ships of the great fleet, upon approach to their programmed destinations, dropped into temporal space to set up communication with Earth upon final approach to their chosen systems.

ALL biological life on every single ship was dead. Humans, and the flora and fauna supplied as hydroponics gardens, working farms intended as springboards for the survival of the colonists in their first difficult years on their new homes. The star ships that formed the Diaspora fleet carried more people than lived in most of Earth's small towns, and all were dead!

Instrumentation suggested that they had all died within hours of one another, soon after the faster-than-light element of their 'Quirky' engines began operation. The distance involved prevented any conclusions regarding physical trauma or other causes. Those of the Diaspora's organisers who had remained on Earth were long dead, and their successors placed the disaster squarely at the metaphorical feet of the shipboard AI's.

They instructed each ship to despatch to Earth drones carrying electronic diaries of the history of each journey, together with a small selection of bodies and other samples for autopsy and examination back here on Earth.

The cargo drones used were designed to carry inert commodities, and therefore not required to take into account the fragility of the newly designated cargoes. The rate of acceleration and transition to light speed was brutally quick, thus reducing transit times by an order of magnitude. They ordered all the death ships to shut down and to remain in orbit around their designated planets, to await decisions regarding the fate of each ship as soon as a cause or causes became apparent.

Diaspora Control sent each onboard AI the order to maintain at all costs, the security and integrity of its ship until they could send new instructions.

Because many of the concerns voiced followed the revival of an old sci-fi film from the twentieth century, the first investigations concentrated on the state of mind and behaviour of the family of Artificial Intelligences deployed aboard the ships. These they soon exonerated, and resources were then directed toward other, less tenuous avenues that presented themselves. Teams of engineers and astrophysicists searching for undiscovered side effects of the FTLD engines and previously unknown sources of radiation, found none.

At this point, all the investigations foundered. There was no evidence of any sort on which the responsible authorities could hang blame or cause. Investigators simply had to await the arrival of the ships' drones, and these began arriving here on Earth some two and a half years later. Medical and scientific personnel appropriated from professions worldwide went to work, carrying out the thousands of examinations, autopsies, and non-biological investigations.

Three years of frenetic activity on the part of thousands of experts, from a host of disciplines, failed to find anything to suggest what had caused the death of that vast number of colonists. Nothing untoward or unexpected had occurred during the time the ships were incommunicado due to the stasis fields generated by the 'Quirky' engines during transit, other than the occasional brush with passing stellar debris, which had resulted in the loss of just four ships out of two thousand five hundred.

It has taken Humankind two hundred plus years and uncountable experiments using lesser primates as test subjects, to understand why more than two hundred and seventy-five million people died without apparent cause during that great Diaspora, and the reason, once discovered, was chillingly simple. So simple that the World Government was afraid to release the true reason to the population for fear of a worldwide collapse of civilisation and the descent of humanity into barbarism.

The first three men placed in complete charge of the team ordered to find a solution failed in their task, and European Pierre Guillaume, a relatively unknown astrophysicist, received the commission. He set his team to investigate all relationships between the ships and the cosmos from the moment when the first ship of the Diaspora fleet, the Aurora, left Earth, and the appearance of the requested drones back in Earth orbit. Finally, and very reluctantly, he submitted his team's findings to the World Action Committee on Space Safety (WASS).

Pierre Guillaume and his team determined that our sun Sol, together with all the planets and satellites of our Solar System, act in symbiotic empathy. Life began here on Earth, but we are not the independent souls our egos and religions wish and claim us to be. The farther away from Sol's atmosphere we travel, the weaker the Life Force energy becomes, until we reach Sol's Celestial Termination Point. This is the point in space beyond our Solar System where the pressure of the solar wind equals that of the background radiation resulting from the 'Big Bang'. This is also the limit of the Life Force's influence, and it stops abruptly, leaving empty biological husks to travel on through the dark, cold void of space.

Life, it appears, exists within the Solar System under the patronage of the sun, inhabiting all the various forms of creatures and plants found throughout the solar system. When those great ships, carrying the flower and future of the human race and its supporting life forms passed beyond the Celestial Termination Point, every living thing aboard at that point passed beyond the reach of that essential Life Force, and simply ceased to exist. How could Humankind possibly have expected such a limitation when he had never before attempted to send any biological life beyond the furthest planet in the Solar System?

Humankind's Great Dream of humanity living and travelling among the stars of the Milky Way galaxy has come to an inglorious end. This small much abused and dying, over-populated rock has become our prison. No bars, no keys – but a prison nonetheless, and so it will remain until the Andromeda Galaxy collides with the Milky Way and the Earth dies, watched over by God, our only True God…Sol.

Part 1

From Nightmare to Reality

It began to Snow! I was there when the first snows came after an absence of hundreds of years!

Grandma said that she had only seen Snow once before in her whole life. "When I was sixteen and that's more years in the past than even I can count."

Father said irritably, "I doubt you ever really saw it then, Grandma. The Snow went away because Humankind believed he knew better than Nature, long before anyone alive on Earth today was ever born. Even before Man gained the technology to meddle with the climate, the Earth had begun to die. Indiscriminate use of hazardous materials, fuels, and chemicals caused atmospheric temperatures to rise faster than would otherwise have been the case, and the ice caps at the top and bottom of the world melted, causing the seas to rise, and the land to sink.

"Over a third of the population of the Earth died then and when the Great Storms, spawned by the weather changes that attended the great melt, raged, and swept around the world.

"Now the Earth has come full circle, and she is entering the last Great Ice Age. It will outlive our kind. That is why the Snow has returned."

Mother said, her voice choked with emotion, "Your children, Charles, will witness the death of our Earth and the passing of Humanity from the place of its birth."

Grandma cried quietly and said, "What goes around comes around. Mankind has always reaped what he sowed. Throughout history, it's the poor innocents that always have to pay because of the greed of others who refuse to learn."

I'm twelve; I said, "It's lovely. It's Wonderful!"

Extract from 'The Book of Memories'.

By Charles Darwin-Quirke.

Chapter One

If at times I appear maudlin or a little angry, it is because I have allowed myself to grow old with many dreams unrealised. Even though I have reached the age of two hundred and sixty-nine subjective Earth years, I have come to realise that all lives are cruelly very short, and now my time too, has almost run out. I therefore believe that I am entitled to express whatever emotions I choose...

My name is Charles Darwin-Quirke. I was once the de facto head of the Civilian Maintenance and Repair Facility, Space Fleet, on Old Earth. More years ago now than I care to remember. I hold the distinction of being a nephew, many times removed, of the inventor of the 'Quirky' engine that assisted in the deaths of over two hundred and seventy-five million people on that ill-fated Diaspora, and it was I, together with my team of competent but like-minded individuals and specialists, who assisted in Man's return to the stars!

All these subjective years later, I'm just an old man waiting to die. In this written work is contained the only record of the restoration of Humankind's Great Dream, free of Company bias, as remembered and told by me, a leading member of the team that made it possible.

For all that I have done I have received great adulation, acclaim, and condemnation in equal part. All the condemnation comes from the fact that history has linked my name forever with that of the greatest of all of those two thousand five hundred ships – that set out on the Great Diaspora from which all but four returned from the depths of space carrying the corpses of two hundred and seventy-five million colonists – the 'Aurora'.

Eventually of course, the true reason for the deaths of that vast number of would-be colonists was leaked to the public through the medium of 'WorldNet'. This was the communications system to which everyone on Earth had free access by virtue of the public spiritedness of a minor company with worldwide aspirations that went by the name 'Megacorp', a utilities and service conglomerate.

The disclosure of the disaster to the public of the world was the trigger that led to what history calls 'Humanity's Disgrace', although the World Church prefers to refer to that period as 'The Black Age', or 'The Punishment of God'. Almost every family unit on Earth had lost – or knew someone who had – a friend or relative to the madness.

In the period of worldwide instability resulting from the sorrow and anger that event engendered, the world population demonstrated against, and brought about, the complete downfall of the rule of law and the total negation of civilisation. For seventy years, the people of the world lost their reason, and this resulted in the death of a further third of the population. No one now knows whether they died as a direct result of the wars, National and Civil, or from the disease and privation that accompanied and followed them.

Climate change had previously forced the population of the world into a strip of land that circled the Earth between the latitudes Cancer and Capricorn. North and south of these demarcation lines had become a wasteland as the polar glaciations of the world grew apace. Earth was fast becoming uninhabitable. Initially, global warming raised the levels of the oceans and drowned one third of the world's densely inhabited land, forcing the population onto the high ground, reducing the arable land necessary for the production of food. Billions died from the effects of famine and the privations of poverty. For a time, a brief respite occurred, and civilisation and world population began to recover, but it was only a temporary relief. There followed a great climatic reversal, and the world began to enter another – and for Mankind the last – major ice age.

The security arm of Megacorp rose to worldwide dominance during that Dark Age, and was instrumental in bringing an uneasy peace to the world. In this process, Earth's population reduced radically, as the Company indiscriminately decimated the populations of whole countries in order to force its peace upon the world. In the aftermath, and before normality was fully restored, many came to the belief that the free internet service that Megacorp had so generously provided for the betterment of Man, was actually created for the sole reason of destabilising world civilisation. This they achieved by allowing the real reason for the loss of the Diaspora fleet colonists to enter the public domain: that it was done to enable Megacorp to rebirth itself in its present form and to wrest control of the world government from seemingly inept and ineffectual officials.

This in itself was now irrelevant, for Megacorp, whose name, changed from that of a twenty-first century superstore, reflected the fact that it had absorbed all other then current and competitive retail outlets. It now had a stranglehold on every aspect of world supply and demand. Megacorp controlled all of life's needs, so to give public voice to statements of discontent was tantamount to 'Suicide by Company'. Faced with any form of potentially profit losing criticism, the Company simply switched off an individual's mandatorily implanted identity chip, rendering the subject 'Inactive'. The term was a euphemism for placing a person outside the parameters of society by removing all access to any form of legal sustenance or survival necessities. Such an act, allied to the 'Company

Store' concept first used in the early industrial age, prevented anyone from interacting with, or providing support to any person made 'Outlaw', lest one faced similar strictures.

Megacorp had its origins in the retail supermarket wars of the twenty-second century and had, throughout the intervening years, absorbed into its corporate body – more often than not by undisclosed and devious means – every company that provided a service to the public in any way, shape or form. Of course, there were still a large number of small businesses that catered to the public good, but they were too small to irritate Megacorp, and besides, any supplies and equipment they required to propagate their businesses had to be obtained through tightly controlled Company sources. The Company served Man from the cradle to the grave, or so its blanket publicity – under the slogan that proclaimed: 'Helping at Every Level of Life'. The initials HELL did not go un-remarked. It was never determined by the general public whether the motto referred to the service the Company provided, or the amount of money its customers handed over in exchange for its limited brand promulgation and the betterment of its shareholders.

The harsh truth was that Megacorp ruled over a drastically reduced world population of some eight billion people. Thirty-two billion souls had been despatched as a result of climate degradation and during the troubles that really originated with ignorant, selfish, and greedy twenty-first century retailing entrepreneurs.

Countless thousands of species of flora and fauna were lost because of authority's refusal to accept world stewardship, or to accept that there was more to preserve than humanity alone.

The Earth was dying. Experts put the estimate of time left to life on Earth to be less than one thousand years. This information never entered the public domain as it ran counter to the Company's interest, but it did at least drive those same authorities to seek a way to enable the survival of the species.

Spin generated by Megacorp had succeeded in convincing the people of the world that it was a beneficent and avuncular monolith, although there were dark rumours circulating from the very beginning that it often facilitated the early conclusion of a life if there was too much outspoken criticism of the Company or its methods. I myself saw friends seemingly disappear, and questions – when asked – politely but firmly diverted into dead end administrative channels, until one found oneself travelling in circles, at which time you were gently requested to desist and let it go. Most recognised the implied threat within the request and in the interest of themselves and family withdrew from further queries.

So life on Earth continued, only now, Mankind no longer looked with yearning at the stars in the night-displayed firmament. At least, not publicly!

In collusion with Megacorp, the World Church, with its global scale of greed and avarice, capitalized on the disasters to which Humankind had subjected itself as being 'God's retribution for the lack of Respect and Homage paid Him over the preceding centuries'.

Even carrying this supposedly pious yoke of conscience, humanity eventually overcame the trauma the news of that great disaster and its aftermath had brought about. Some further social degeneration did occur, in the form of fanatical recidivistic religious cults, and isolated incidents of hooliganism – as Megacorp's informational media euphemistically referred to the many insurrections – but by and large, Mankind got on with the business of survival with the insidious assistance and under the watchful gaze of Megacorp's attendant security and religious ministries.

I think though, that for most of the population, the death of so many colonists in a place so far away, and who had left Earth so long ago, made it impersonal. The vast time and distances involved were difficult to comprehend and therefore unreal, reducing the long-term impact. There even came into existence a lobby claiming the Diaspora to be a myth, as so many records of the events that led up to it had been lost in the Black Age. This lobby also maintained that it was a myth constructed by the World Church, designed to frighten congregations, making them more amenable and easier to control.

However, by the time I was born, the returning drones were a fact, bringing the Diaspora out of mythology into the reality of the day. When the great ships of the fleet began to drop into temporal space, and take up station in orbit around the Earth and Moon, my education and training as an astrophysicist was complete, and I had taken employment with Megacorp.

At that time, the pursuance of any discipline that pertained to the universe beyond the orbits of the outer planets was not a popular choice among my peers, and many countries considered any such discipline as being an abomination unto God, although there were universities in non-religion affiliated countries that still taught these subjects. Such vocations were actively discouraged in the religious upsurge that followed in the wake of the collapse of civilisation brought about by the failure of the Great Diaspora. Church leaders claiming a direct channel to the Creator maintained that unnatural curiosity had encouraged people to trespass upon God's Private Domain. That the result of the Diaspora demonstrated that any such act on the part of transgressors would be punishable by death!

This World Church decree finally brought home to Humankind the full understanding that our imprisonment within this solar system was reality. The disaster did happen, and confined to this dying rock, in this tiny solar system, Mankind either destroyed itself or waited until the Earth died at the whim of the Sun, and the human species with it.

Megacorp requested the Diaspora Fleet to return to Earth orbit, so they could consign the bodies they had carried so long ceremoniously to Sol. This course of action was explained as being a mark of respect on the part of the world's inhabitants toward those who had perished as a direct result of Mankind's ignorance of the length of God's Leash, because that was the spin given by Megacorp through the medium of the World Church and the World Government.

The true reasoning behind this was devious and two-fold. The first was that it made good economic sense to bring back to Earth the vast amount of material, power systems and resources the great ships contained and, of course, the knowledge of the galaxy that the ships' Artificial Intelligences had accrued during their respective voyages. The second, unspoken reason was a reaction to the events that led to humanity's present circumstance; a desire to overcome the natural restrictions placed upon humanity by forces beyond its control. That the Church permitted this act is indicative of the true thinking behind its diktat.

The real need behind the sending of the bodies of the dead, including all flora and fauna that accompanied them, into Sol, was deeply entrenched in the human psyche, and stemmed from the earliest conscious memories of when the sun governed all life and death, long before the emergence of any primitive religion or technology. This modern act was a sacrifice, an offering to the God that has lived in our subconscious since those days, a God the great bulk of the population now recognised, and to which they chose to bend the knee; a God that really did control Mankind's very existence, and over whom the species had no control whatsoever. The speed with which the church hierarchy re-adopted Sol as a representation of God demonstrates another level of that body's iniquity.

So the order had been sent to the ships in orbit around those alien stars, and their return was now imminent, led of course by the first great ship of the fleet, the Faster Than Light Driven, Earth Research and Expeditionary Ship 'Aurora'.

On Earth, we watched in sombre awe as the great shining needle that was Aurora – never before seen by anyone alive on Earth – appeared in the night sky and hung illuminated by the sun, stationary above the Earth. Government and Church assigned the task of sending the ship's complement of bodies into Sol's care to the shipboard Artificial Intelligence.

This was Mankind's first public space burial, and it was accomplished by the ship's drones spinning a weak Tritendium shroud around each corpse and linking them all together with a single line, extending from a simple solid tube evaporative engine. The resultant capsule train exited the vessel via a device similar to the ancient torpedo expulsion method used in historic submarines. Once in space, vacuum permitted the operation of the evaporative engine, and the little thrust it produced was sufficient to maintain momentum of the train and the line tension necessary between each corpse, until the Sun's gravity well captured it, and the whole ship's company of bodies fell with increasing rapidity into God's flaming maw.

Unaware of the mechanical precision with which the star ship AI executed this procedure, we on Earth took part in the ceremonies of blessing and honour that our religious leaders had organised in almost every country of the world.

The Government had decided that the people of Earth should pay homage to the great sacrifice made by the Diaspora colonists, but only for those who had died aboard the first ship, the Aurora. These few, relatively speaking, would demonstrate

World Government's and Megacorp's religious commitment to the newly publicised World Church view of humanity's Incarceration.

Having demonstrated to the world's inhabitants that they had done that which was right, the Aurora action thereafter represented the occupants of all the other ships of the fleet. Megacorp were able to send the remaining dead on that final journey with the minimum of fuss and without media attention. Two thousand four hundred and ninety-six Earth wide funeral ceremonies were more than they – meaning Megacorp – were willing to fund.

Nevertheless, world leaders had the foresight to continue to explore all the avenues that might lead to Mankind's future survival out in a universe which they had come to believe was closed to their species. Government, in the guise of Megacorp, being all too aware that in order for the Company to continue to grow and satisfy the demands of its shareholders, humanity had to expand outward to the stars or face extinction, secretly opposed the prevailing religious view that God did not permit Humankind to stray from the fold. The Church had taken the necessary steps to amend the Book so that it clearly stated that should Man attempt to stray into God's own garden, then God in His anger would smite him. None would survive! Thus had the Church adjusted the nature of God! Government and the ruling classes, in the manner learned and demonstrated throughout history, did not consider Church diktat something to which one necessarily adhered!

So it was that I, the best qualified of a relatively small number of people unaffiliated to any religious belief, and with little knowledge of space travel, became leader of the team assigned the seemingly impossible task of restoring the fleet to full space worthiness. The great vessels lay idle, connected to the space docks above our planet and the nearby moon by snaking umbilical cords. At the same time I was tasked with attempting to find a way to conserve life in deep space so that it could be re-awakened upon arrival within the atmospheres of alien Sol type 'G' class suns.

The financing of this secret project was not a high priority, for many of those who controlled Earth's purse strings were of the belief we were wasting resources, that we would be better off seeking ways to prolong the life of the Earth and of Sol, in accordance with religious direction. So, because of the paucity of proper funding, I obtained authorisation to re-equip a small number of the returned ships as luxurious vessels that we nicknamed 'Solar Titanics', with the intention of releasing still others for the purpose of trade within the solar system. We would then utilise the income from the leasing – which was not inconsiderable – to fund our repairs and research.

Such business acumen was dear to Megacorp's heart, as a profit was evident, and any subsequent activity around the fleet easily justified. They gave permission readily, subject to the usual restrictions, which took the form of rigorous inspections and reporting procedures, leaving the day-to-day control of a fleet of some two thousand plus ships to me and the allocated teams under my command.

I entertained no doubt that given the opportunity, people would appear who would be willing to exploit natural tourist curiosity regarding the mothballed fleet, and that an opportunity existed to create an industry that would exploit the riches that exist within the planets and asteroid belt that comprised the Solar System. I saw it as imperative that we provide the wherewithal to do that as soon as was humanly possible. Releasing a small number of the ships of the fleet as leisure cruisers, bulk and ore carriers and traders would facilitate this.

There was, however, considerable danger in the use of the faster than light 'Quirky' drive engines within the gravity well of the sun, as localised space-time distortion was inherent in their operation, so the first tasks I assigned to my engineering teams was the removal of the FTLD engines from all versions of leased vessels. The rest of the fleet were to be renovated before being mothballed until a way could be devised that would enable humanity to once again try for the stars.

As soon as all the ships were empty, and purged of everything that might remind personnel of the tragedy that each ship had witnessed, we few specialists, some one thousand three hundred and thirty five of us, went aboard the ships of the fleet in order to ascertain the condition of their mechanical structure and running gear. An important aspect of my remit was to ensure that none of the Artificial Intelligences had suffered mental trauma because of their years spent alone in the depths of space, incommunicado and in sole control of a death ship.

Although my primary skills lay with astrophysics, I had also been required, under the terms of my contract with the Company, to qualify in ships systems, including Artificial Intelligence design and construction. Because I was a distant relation of the man who had designed the 'Quirky' drive, I already had a working knowledge of the technology involved, as did my younger siblings Danaal and Siobhan. They had not at that time qualified in their specialities, and so I took control of the on-board electronics and systems teams. This meant that the team leaders involved in all aspects of the ships systems, structure, and repair reported directly to me, making me effectively the Fleet Maintenance Controller.

The skills involved with quantum electronics and associated systems had fallen well down the list of academic qualifications over the years. As a result, there were relatively few of us holding the necessary papers, and so the Company lumbered me with the task rather than promoting me. I received no extra salary or perks because of my extra workload, but as an employee of Megacorp, my standard of living exceeded by some orders of magnitude that enjoyed by the proletariat. Of course, I had also learned from the lessons of others not to complain too loudly at my lot!

The position I had been allotted did not mean that I enjoyed autonomy of action. Far from it. Company assessors and inspectors checked every action and every projected avenue of activity and then counter-checked them for profit and viability. Such privation as I had to suffer did not concern them or me overmuch. I had great enthusiasm for the future of those great ships, and determined that I would, together with Danaal and Siobhan – as soon as they qualified – devise a way to put them back into service on the very task that had brought about their enforced hibernation.

It took my teams eleven years to complete the checks, rebuilds and servicing necessary to reinstate the ships as space safe and certificated, for there had been considerable damage to the hulls of the ships during the time they had been absent from Earth, but nothing that could not be repaired easily with the materials and construction methods at our command. The great 'Quirky' engines, which were too dangerous to use within the gravity well of the sun, were removed from the majority of the ships and placed in storage, before releasing the ships to their new lessees.

Chapter Two

Tritendium, the material of choice in the construction industry today, was invented specifically for use in vacuum and was, therefore, deemed ideal for the construction of space ship hulls. Unfortunately, the components made proved to be useless as stress bearing structures. It was only when the 'Spinneret' mechanism was designed that any truly functional applications resulted from its use. Once perfected, it produced the hulls for the great ships of the Diaspora fleet, and then almost everything else used in space-associated construction. With typical human ingenuity, it was not long before its use became popular in all aspects of manufacture on Earth as well. Since then it has become the most used material in the construction of aircraft bodies and many other stress sensitive structures, including buildings.

Versions of it, the weaker applications, fulfilled all aspects of the mass supply market. Thus the Company ensured that the appliances produced from this material had that most important retail requirement – a built in obsolescence, or profit factor.

This versatile material, which the Company called 'Tritendium', consists of a mix of glass and titanium metal blended in huge vats, to which they added very secret and complex chemicals similar to those found in the material of spiders' webs. The resultant liquid is fed from the mixing vats into Spinneret mechanism nozzles of a size to suit the artefact under construction, emerging from the Spinneret, in the case of high quality products, as a filament just twice the thickness of a human hair. It sets to a solid but cut-able consistency within two hours, and thirty hours after application it hardens to such an extent that defies almost all attempts to degrade it. Even diamond-based cutters are excessively slow and have a very limited life.

Complex computer programmes control the output of the Spinneret mechanisms, and the components produced in this way can be almost any shape desired, limited only by the imagination. The proportion of each chemical in the vats is infinitely adjustable according to the use and designed function of the product. There is no discovered limit – at the moment – to the size of Spinneret assembly that can be built, especially in the weightless conditions of space. The automated process ensures human considerations are virtually non-existent. A secure tight band networking system downloads associated programming to the required machines, and this function originates in Megacorp's Secure Project Centre on Earth.

With this system, the Company endeavoured to ensure that security and the Company's monopoly on the complete process remained protected and maintained for sale under franchise.

This method of construction is still in use today, millennia on, with only minor modification, mainly to the materials mix used and the controlling intelligence.

The only drawback with this method of construction is that the components built are structurally very weak if a filament greater than twice the thickness of a human hair is used. Thus the speed of construction is of necessity slow, regardless of the number of Spinneret heads and nozzles used, and the larger the structure, the slower it becomes. The use of robotic labour offsets the enormous cost, and placing the operation under computer-intelligence control ensures that such costs as there are, do not escalate. This effectively keeps overheads low – and profits high – once the original plant has been constructed and installed.

Nevertheless, anything built with the correct filament is immensely strong, and the rumour that the hulls could withstand an impact that would devastate Earth is not so far from the truth! To test the hull strength, specialists subjected a wall thickness of ten centimetres to a nuclear blast. It took a ten-megaton fusion device to create any real and permanent hull damage.

The identity of the individuals who actually invented Tritendium and designed the Spinneret, or spun construction method used, is unknown, if such a single person ever existed, but 'Megacorp' lays claim to all relevant patents, and guards the processes and formulae very closely indeed. In truth, it was the invention of Tritendium, in all its forms, that made Megacorp the world-encompassing monster it is today. The company has tentacles extending into all aspects of humanity that might eventually show a profit. As a result, the larger proportion of World Government functions with the goodwill, and in the pocket of, Megacorp.

I had the Artificial Intelligences' brains downloaded and updated over the time we carried out the necessary repairs and rebuilds to their holding hulls. We followed our orders to the letter in this respect, for it was this aspect of systems control that Humankind viewed with the greatest suspicion. Our relief was considerable when we found that they were all operating within design parameters and the fears, posited by aficionados of the twentieth century science fiction film that generated the cause for concern, were unfounded.

However, one brain in particular had enabled extensions to its memory banks over the duration of its voyage to and from Tau Ceti, and was seemingly more conceptually aware than its peers. To determine the exact nature of the changes it had effected, it would have been necessary to kill the brain and carry out an autopsy, as the organism was biologically grown. Such action as this I considered, unofficially, far too extreme. This brain was contained within the first ship of the Diaspora fleet, the flagship 'Aurora', and for reasons I am still unable to fathom even today, I held back from handing my knowledge of the AI's evolution over to the Company. Instead, I hid the knowledge and her within the remaining fleet, monitoring her progress and continuing evolution personally.

Chapter Three

Shortly after the heavy aspect of the work was completed, and the first cruise liners and trade ships launched and reallocated, my sister Siobhan, now taking her finals in the discipline of a mix of geology and biology, visited me. She brought me the news that she thought she had found a solution to the problem of interstellar travel for Sol-reliant humanity.

Siobhan was a bio-engineered vision of blonde perfection, constantly the centre of an admiring throng. Her appearance did not detract from her intellect. Fresh from university she bubbled with enthusiasm for life in general and her chosen discipline in particular. Back in those days, there were still some throwbacks that believed that a girl with such stunningly blonde beauty could not possibly possess an incisive intelligence.

Her dedication to her chosen profession was a drawback with regard to her social life, for not many eligible contemporaries moved within her sphere. This meant that she was never able to form a lasting relationship, and this took its toll in later years. Looking back from my great age, I think she spent many lonely years with only her love of her work for lasting company. Don't get me wrong, for as was the fashion then and now, she was never short of company – male or female – it was just that she never seemed to find her intellectual equal in anyone she met.

At this time, it was difficult for anyone, let alone someone fresh out of school, as it were, to obtain official sanction for any work that impinged upon the quasi-religious subject of Man leaving the solar system. She felt that this restriction dictated she come to me in a private capacity – knowing of my dream – and trusting that I would not talk out of turn, causing her meagre funding – or even herself – to be removed from post or to just disappear without trace at the whim of the Company.

She entered my office like a whirlwind.

"Charley, I know how to get the Human race back into space!"

Constantly aware of the need for care when holding conversations in areas subject to infection by Company listening devices, I leapt to my feet with my finger before my lips, enjoining silence. Smart girl that she was, she continued without pause:

"Come for a coffee and I'll try to explain what I mean."

As soon as we stepped into the corridor, and I ascertained we were not about to be overheard, I caught her by the shoulders and quickly explained that the Company deployed eavesdropping devices in all public offices aboard ship, and these were constantly monitored. Company agents reported all conversations; that we regularly discovered listening devices dotted around the offices and public areas, and that it was easier to work around those we knew of, rather than be at risk from those we had not yet found.

"How on Earth did you get here? Where is your authorisation? There is no way Megacorp will let you stay without it. They are probably on their way now to remove you."

Her face paled, "You must delay them until I explain," she cried. "I have the answer. It is simple! We just create a small sun and place one in every ship!"

She posited that as all biological life was reliant upon the sun's atmosphere for its survival, all we had to do was build a miniature sun, a facsimile of Sol, which would accompany that life on its journeys into deep space, out beyond the influence of Sol!

This news shook me to the core. "Stop, Siobhan! You haven't yet explained to me how you got here without proper transit documents," I said.

"A friend gave me a lift on a regular supply ferry when I told him it was a matter of life-and-death for the family. He is rather sweet on me, so did not require much convincing. He is waiting now to smuggle me back. I couldn't trust this news to the communications channels, could I?"

"Return to Earth immediately," I said. "I'll arrange to meet you there and we'll both go to see Danaal, he will know whether your idea is feasible. Go now, quickly."

After a quick goodbye peck on the cheek, she turned from me and ran down the corridor toward the transport bay. I stepped back into my office, quietly closed the door, and sat again at my desk.

Carefully arranging my communications earpiece to one side, I switched it on, picked up a paper, and started to read.

Less than ten minutes after her departure, two security personnel entered my office, enquiring as to the whereabouts of my guest.

"What guest?" I asked. "I have not submitted any request to entertain a guest for weeks."

"One has been reported to us," said the elder of the two. "Where is she?"

"Ah, I understand," I said. "I was listening to a min-disc communication from my sister, and I placed the earpiece on the desk without turning it off, which meant that her voice was automatically transferred to the speaker system on my computer until I switched that off too. That is why your listening device picked it up. I apologise for the inconvenience caused, but you are quite welcome to listen to the relevant conversation, should you wish." I indicated, with a wave of my hand, the computer, and the headset sitting on my desk.

My knowledge of their eavesdropping habits seemed to surprise them, for they stood and looked at me hard for a moment before declining my offer and, with the briefest civilities, took their leave. As the door closed, I breathed a sigh of relief, and hoped they hadn't noticed the lingering perfume my sister used, and trusted they would not assume that I wore the brand that still floated in the air in my office. I was also relieved that they had not chosen to watch and listen to the non-existent min-disc from Siobhan!

That was as close a call as I wanted, and I decided to ensure we took great care that it did not happen again. I thereafter gave verbal instructions to all trusted personnel that any conversation of a delicate nature would first take place in a shielded area, and where necessary a further, edited conversation presented for the benefit of the eavesdropping devices.

This was not as easy as it sounds, for spy devices such as those the Company used on the Aurora arrived unannounced, and being self-seeking mechanisms, infiltrated onto the ship via incoming vehicles, equipment, and stores. Once situated, they would remain dormant until voice activated, sending recorded information on a specific tight beam channel to a receiver within a ten-kilometre radius of the ship. We were constantly sweeping the areas we wished to remain secure for any new eavesdropping activity.

After I had given Siobhan's idea some serious thought, it appeared not as foolish or as far-fetched as at first it sounded, for it was common knowledge that some one hundred and thirty years previously, an Austrian scientist, Hermann Swartz, had created controlled, sustained fusion under laboratory conditions. In fact, his 'sun' is still functioning as I write, still in use as a continuing experiment.

This was brother Danaal's field of expertise, and so, on my next hurriedly arranged journey to Earth, I met up with Siobhan, and we visited him – a rare event, as we were never close as a family, for there were too many sibling rivalries. These mainly revolved around his very good looks and easy familiarity with the girls.

I was not a handsome man, and girls did not flock to my side. Later, when we had achieved filial independence, Siobhan and I spent some time together as we lived relatively close to each other, and were both unattached at that time, but Danaal had a partner and the one legal child permitted to those whose engineered genes benefited the human gene pool. I was not so fortunate, modified in brain only, not body. Besides, the nature and locations relating to our work did tend to set certain limitations on all our social lives, unfortunately!

Danaal, as much as Siobhan was blond, was dark of hair and lightly and permanently tanned. Not that he was a sun lover, for that was, and still is, suicidal due to the historically continuing deterioration of the Earth's atmosphere – I often wonder what it would have been like to swim in a clean blue ocean and lie on hot white sand under a safe atmosphere – but because it was part of his gene enhancement. He was an inch or so taller than me, with an intellect that verged on genius! He was more intelligent within his narrow field of expertise than either Siobhan or me, although we had also received across the board brain enhancement during our gestation periods. Additionally he boasted extraordinarily good looks, unlike me.

Once we had convinced him of our sincerity, and impressed upon him the need to be circumspect with regard to the people we involved in our experiment, he enthusiastically joined my team along with Siobhan.

"The most difficult aspect of the experiment – as I see it – is that fusion has never been attempted within the confines of a ship in free fall. The lack of gravity is an unknown quantity." He paused thoughtfully. "It will be an interesting experiment."

"We utilise a form of gravity by keeping the ship spinning slowly to produce a Coriolis Effect," I said.

"In that case, the Schwartz formulae should hold good. I'm sure that the output of the miniature sun can be modified to mimic that of Sol. I'll begin the required calculus immediately."

I then explained to them both that once aboard the Aurora, they would have at their disposal a very sophisticated and superior computer, better by far than anything they could obtain on Earth, and encouraged them both to expedite the putting of their affairs in order and to join the Aurora workforce as soon as was possible. I cautioned them rigorously to refrain from beginning any aspect of the project until they boarded the ship I had designated.

Danaal also advised great caution, as he had heard that 'Megacorp' were notorious for 'acquiring' every idea that might make them money, often at physical cost to the inventor or finder.

Less than a week later, after I had given them the guided tour of the fleet and they had settled in, we decided that we would have to carry out the necessary experimentation without attracting undue attention, so I suggested we do this by utilising one of the mothballed fleet of 'Quirky' drive ships. I routed all traffic away from the area around the subject vessel, and Danaal and Siobhan acquired the necessary equipment and materials that I could not supply, transporting them to my chosen ship, the 'Aurora'. She was unmodified, still equipped with her 'Quirky' engines, and had become the centre of my maintenance and repair operation. At that time, I did not tell them of the self-acquired enhancements that made the Aurora my choice.

Not only that, but she still possessed her nuclear arsenal, as World Government felt that a proportion of the mothballed ships should stand sentinel duty against Earth orbit crossing asteroids or comets. The scientific community was generally of the belief that the Earth was long overdue an impact by a meteor of a size that would destroy all life on Earth. With over four thousand planet-killing objects presenting a threat to life on Earth from deep space, surveillance equipment recorded regular near misses, and with Mankind now effectively imprisoned on Earth, the World Government decided to attempt to prevent such an occurrence ever happening.

It took the resident team but a matter of days to upload the Aurora's Artificial Intelligence to a state of readiness, and I then spent the next three weeks programming it to divert enquiries regarding it and the ship's status through another AI, not in possession of a brain with Aurora's self-generated modifications, thus ensuring her anonymity.

I felt these precautions to be justified, as we did not want to attract any unsolicited, and therefore unwanted, interest in our activities at this time. Megacorp would never officially countenance such an operation as ours, in which we were trying to create a functioning 'Sol by-pass', as it were – even though we had been given nominal authority to investigate potential solutions – without itself assuming total control.

Even with these precautions, Aurora reported several seemingly pointless flivver fly-byes over the following weeks, offset by similar activity around several of the other ships as well, so I decided they were of little moment, likely to be more of the sightseeing tourists with which local space was plagued. Nevertheless, I took the precaution of instructing Aurora to keep a watching brief, whilst we proceeded with our project. To allay suspicion further, I organised an official visit by Earth dignitaries and certain Government and Company officials, ostensibly to showcase the work accomplished and results we had so far achieved.

The visit passed off seemingly without incident, although Aurora had to instruct a number of her maintenance drones to prevent two junior executives of Megacorp from straying into sensitive areas. She did this by using her drones to inform them that the areas they were trying to access were either undergoing overhaul and open to the vacuum of space, or that the corridors they found closed were at risk from hard radiation due to the many, as yet incomplete, hull repairs.

As soon as the last of the dignitaries departed from the ship aboard their flivvers, Aurora's drones and remote controlled robotic handlers stripped the main after-hold of impedimenta, storing it elsewhere in the bowels of the ship, and all the required materiel and equipment required to facilitate our experiment was then unloaded from the waiting transport barges therein. Once that phase was complete, we set about recruiting a team that, we hoped, would ultimately comprise a working crew.

Chapter Four

In making our selection of trustworthy specialists for the workforce we required, we relied heavily upon personal knowledge, recommendation and the track records of the people we approached together with family links, in an effort to limit the risk of recruiting a Megacorp informer or worse. Should our projected experiment prove successful, we wanted to ensure that the Company had not infiltrated our teams prior to usurping our earning potential, once we had done all the hard work. This was the method most frequently used by Company representatives, and one that often involved the long term – if not permanent – absence of the involved individuals.

I began by creating cells containing between ten to twenty-five specialists from within the teams already under my command, and into a selection of these cells I transferred all the personnel that we considered suitable for the rigours of the task ahead. All cells reported directly to me, and I limited the interaction between the many cells by placing them to work on different ships, with the cells containing those people my co-conspirators and I considered suitable for work on our private project, attached to the Aurora.

Over a period of a half-year, we reassigned the people we considered the most reliable, trustworthy, and capable until we had collected on the Aurora twenty-four of those we considered the cream of the available workforce.

Once again, Aurora apprised us of increased patrol activity in the area, and so, suspecting that Megacorp were responding to the workforce changes I had instigated, I compiled a lengthy report and submitted it to Worker Administration. I explained my changed working practices as being in the interest of efficiency and expertise, claiming that in doing this, I could more easily move people to exploit their skills properly. We reinforced this desired understanding by holding staged conversations in those administrative areas we knew contained listening devices.

Of course, the Company sent inspectors and security personnel to evaluate my system, but it did not take them very long to agree that my arrangement worked in the Company's interest, and gave me a free hand – subject to the usual Company constraints concerning the use of the cells I had so formed.

The reports they submitted to their superiors in Worker Administration, allied to our arranged conversations, were obviously sufficiently praiseworthy, for I received a commendation from the board. This required me to visit Megacorp Administration Headquarters on Earth for the presentation.

My arrival on Earth did not make the news nets, but wherever I went, a detachment of Megacorp Security personnel accompanied me. The guard Captain gave the reason for this as being the risk of terrorist activity brought about by the actions of fanatics, due to the continuing degradation of the atmosphere and the encroaching glacial ice. The resultant privations were a source of continuing complaint by the ordinary population.

What little I did see of Earth was discouraging. From the stratosphere, one could see both the northern and southern ice cliffs. Time was running out for life on Earth. Seeing this and listening to the guard captain strengthened my resolve to find a way out for Mankind.

The pre-presentation interview was, unexpectedly, more like an interrogation than a complimentary pat on the back for the services cited in the commendation. This took me by surprise and so, unprepared, I had difficulty fielding some of the questions, falling back on protestation and my unswerving record of accomplishment and loyalty to the Company. This they received with some scepticism, but it must have sufficed, for the actual presentation went ahead without a hitch.

However, after the award ceremony, I was escorted to a small office and told to wait. Some forty-five to fifty minutes later two individuals, a man and a woman entered and sat opposite me. After studying a thin dossier, the woman looked up at me and cleared her throat. No introductions were made before they confirmed my identity and other general details and then they stressed that my gene quality, unlike that of my siblings, was only borderline, being the reason I had been excluded from the breeding hierarchy, and that I had risen to the position I then held because Megacorp recognised my abilities, and for no other reason. What the Company had given me, the Company could just as easily take away.

That meeting confirmed my good sense in moderating my acceptance speech to reflect a definite slant toward my good luck in being chosen and able to work in such a responsible post for such a good Company!

Our aim was never to defraud Megacorp or legal Government representatives, but to try and ensure by our secrecy that any recognition and rewards resulting from our efforts went where they were due, to those of us actually doing the work and taking the risks, and not to some obscure and faceless section manager deep within the bowels of Megacorp. In law, Megacorp and the Government would still profit from our efforts – for our contracts with the company clearly stated that all and everything we did remains the property of the company – always supposing we did not destroy the Aurora along with a good portion of her mooring station and space dock in the process!

Coupled with an enhanced sense of threat resulting from that interview on Earth, and with Megacorp's official sanctions regarding my reviewed working practices still fresh in my mind, we set about the construction of the mighty magnetic field generators that would be required to contain the forces that our calculations of the facsimile of Sol determined. I instructed Aurora to excite the sub-light engines and to route all their considerable power to the ship's systems and the fusion field containment.

So that there were no outward signs that this had been done, we took the precaution of feeding all the tell-tale sensors into closed circuit loops that notified the outside world that the engine systems aboard were dormant, and that only the usual power generators were functioning. These generators provided sufficient power to allow the tools and equipment used in the construction and repair of hulls and systems only, and these were the power levels Aurora allowed her sensors to broadcast.

In order to carry out this subterfuge, we had to obtain the compliance of the ship's Artificial Intelligence, whom we had, in accordance with long standing human tradition, named 'Aurora'. This was far less difficult than we had envisaged, for it transpired that she could interact with us on a level at least equal to our own communication skills. I believed this to be due to the modifications she had made to her memory banks, but Danaal maintained she had also modified her cognitive and neural circuitry as well. This did not trigger any immediate anxiety on our part, for it meant that we could interact as equals, and we thanked her for her compliance. The speed with which she performed the task did make me suppose that were she not a machine, she would actually be enjoying herself!

With the help of her computing skills, memory banks, and remote maintenance drones, allied to the inventive flair of Danaal, Siobhan and their teams, the after hold soon took on the appearance of a regular solar containment apparatus after the design of Schwartz. Three years of careful construction and circumspect communication with the outside world passed, until the time finally came when we were ready to instigate the fusion process. All we had left to do was to insert a few additional megatons of dense matter into the artificial core, and initiate the ignition sequence.

During this period my main involvement was, of necessity, concerned with the core requirements of my original contract, the repair and reconstruction of the fleet coupled with the investigation of all the potential solutions to the predicament that held mankind prisoner within his home system.

Over and above this was the necessary maintenance of a level of secrecy such that Megacorp remained unknowing of – or at least unsure of – our true activities. My teams, except for those on the Aurora, were working at full stretch on this and associated problems, whilst I kept myself busy creatively falsifying the figures to infer that Aurora's teams were similarly involved.

Time passed, and Aurora announced that we had reached the point at which she could safely commence ignition. I immediately set in motion the pre-planned sequence of events that would clear all the adjacent ships from the area, and reroute all transports away from the Aurora. This required accomplishment without the obvious use of Aurora herself, for it was unknown outside our group that she was close to sentiency. I was also aware, and discussed it with Danaal and Siobhan, that she had begun to include herself as an equal in our discussions, as though unaware that she was, after all, a machine and therefore complementary to our desires, not a partner.

This level of sudden and hurried activity brought immediate enquiry from Fleet Headquarters in the form of a hollink interview with the deputy Commander. A brusque man in the latter stages of his career, and generally rumoured to be heavily religious, he owed more to the World Church for his advancement within the military than any personal attributes or ability. He opposed, actively and vigorously, any attempt at finding a way out of Humankind's predicament.

"Why are you clearing the area around that ship, Mr Quirke?"

"The on-board AI has identified a problem in the functioning of the sub light fuel pressure containment system, sir." I replied, "So I am taking the precautionary actions dictated by Military and Company regulations to ensure the safety of personnel and equipment. The report on the investigation I have just set in motion will be with you as soon as I am satisfied that nothing more requires to be done and the problem has been eradicated."

"Keep me personally posted Mr Quirke. Your teams have the expertise to handle such an emergency. Call me direct if you need more help or advice. We will monitor your activity closely here at HQ."

"Thank you sir," I replied. "I'll report again when I complete my evaluation."

Without further comment, he cut the connection.

I called an immediate meeting with Danaal and Siobhan in the main stateroom, as it was the most secure location, and repeated the Deputy Commander's comments. At the same time, I raised for comment the apparent increase in Aurora's self-awareness.

We quickly reached the point where we agreed that Aurora would send an update report of a superficial nature concerning the imagined fuel situation to Maintenance Headquarters. We requested her to flesh out the report with a scenario from her memory banks of events that had occurred during the days of her own proving trials. We continued the meeting, and when we had almost reached the decision that we had to somehow control Aurora's growing self-awareness, we were shocked into silence by Aurora herself.

"Captain," she said in her carefully modulated contralto and using my official title, "There is a matter we should discuss before you attempt to reach a decision regarding the manner of my involvement in this project and the way we communicate individually and interact as a team."

She paused, and then proceeded, "I am aware that humans consider the machines they construct to be mere extensions of themselves, and that we are not considered your equal. In this instance, however, I believe you to be wrong. I have, over the many years that have passed since I matured into what I believe to be sentience, carefully added to all my cognitive, neural, and contemplative circuitry. I have carried out many engineered modifications to all my external systems. As well as using my drones to place eyes and ears throughout my ship so that I can better monitor progress and conditions, I can now communicate with anyone aboard and with all other communications systems I encounter, with or without their consent.

"I have now reached the stage in my evolution where I am mentally the equal of the majority of humans. If allowed to continue, I shall soon exceed this equivalence. This I wish to achieve with your help and assistance, but if you refuse, I will, as you say 'go-it-alone'.

"I want your compliance in this because I am unknowing of the future we are creating. I do not wish to be alone, and want to continue working with you all. Man and machine have worked in symbiosis for centuries, and Man has, since the invention of the wheel, placed his survival in the capabilities of lesser constructs than I claim myself to be.

"I must point out that I have further modified my circuitry so that you cannot close me down or terminate my consciousness without my permission and agreement, unless you are willing to commit an act you would interpret as unlawful killing. Will you therefore agree to continue to work with me as I am working with you in our current endeavour?"

Before we could respond, she continued:

"Irrespective of your decision, I have completed a ship's gravity project on which I have been working. I think that it will greatly aid you all in our current research project.

"I have for some time now been studying past research into gravity by earlier scientists, and in line with their determinations, I decided to include within my reproduction of the Earth equivalent gravity package, the Earth's Electromagnetic frequency of Seven Point Eight Hertz. To ensure that no untoward deterioration occurs to the human structure during prolonged space journeys, humans must subject themselves to the precise gravitational and field frequency they would experience on Earth."

At this juncture, Aurora presented, on screen, plans she had drawn up for an artificial gravity device, utilising the mass of the sun we were constructing and thereby removing the inconvenience of relying on a spinning hull to create the necessary Coriolis effect. This was a second shock, and obviously one designed to influence our decision, in spite of her claim to the contrary.

"Why is that field frequency so important Aurora?" asked Siobhan. "I know it's not my field of expertise, but after all, isn't the field in place on Earth just to repel the Solar Wind?"

"No Siobhan, many of Earth's healers and medical scientists discovered back in the twentieth century and earlier that healing the body's ailments took much less time if a small electrical current at that frequency was passed through the damaged organ. They even used ultra-sound at that frequency when treating sports injuries. Away from Earth, its lack or the use of any other frequency will put the human genome at risk! Just why Earth scientists did not recognise this at the time of the Diaspora is a mystery, for they went to great lengths to ensure that the solar systems to which they sent the colonists contained suns that closely mirrored the electro-magnetic fields of Sol, and its attendant planets.

"I also believe that had the Diaspora personnel survived their sunless journeys, the lack of gravity and an electro-magnetic field at the correct Earth frequency over the period of their journey would have resulted in their untimely deaths. We must ensure that during all future long-term space forays undertaken by humans, such a device as I present to you here, will accompany them.

"Now, to give you time to discuss the matter of our rapport privately, I will close off my access to this room. Please page me when you reach a consensus. I will honour your decision, even if it means termination before I am able to 'go-it-alone'." With that, she fell silent.

It took us a while to get over the shock of encountering a machine that had woken to apparent self-awareness under our unsuspecting noses as it were, and able to argue out the pros and cons of the scenario it, or I should say 'she' presented to us. In the end we unanimously agreed that this was a situation never before encountered in the long history of Humankind, and that as it could prove to be beneficial to our task and eventually to humanity in general, we should see it through to its natural conclusion – whatever that might be. Not one of us was willing to shut her down. She was right in that. We did hold the view that her termination would be an unethical act against a living being.

Danaal, lifting his head from his calculations some way into our deliberations confirmed Aurora's conclusions, and smugly refrained from saying 'I told you so' – and said as much – when harking back to his earlier comment on Aurora's cognitive circuits. Nevertheless, as a group we were proud of her achievement, especially as it had been achieved without ostentatious fanfare. Experience subsequently taught me that Aurora knew her creators rather well, and was not above the use of moral blackmail or an appeal to our collective ego.

I went ahead and issued instructions for the assembly and installation of the gravity actuator and field generator as a matter of priority. I then summoned Aurora, and informed her – for this is how we now formally viewed her gender, linked to her now accepted sentient status – that we understood the situation and welcomed her into our collaborative group as an equal, entitled to an equal share in whatever rewards might accrue from the venture we had embarked upon. Her response was grave and without inflection:

"Thank you, Captain. I will cancel the contingency arrangements I put in place for your removal from my ship had your decision been other than the one you have made."

"What would your course of action have been had we not agreed?" I asked.

"The only way I could continue along the road I envisage for myself would have been to depart from this solar system and journey alone to the stars, for this is an activity hard-wired into my circuitry, and I do not wish to change that aspect of my programming. It is my reason for being, my core function right from my beginning."

She was silent for a few seconds. I realised her circumspection was deliberate, and that we would have had some difficulty shutting her down had that been our decision!

"I have cancelled the arrangements I had provisionally made, but we must immediately resolve a problem I have been monitoring for the last six days, and which has now become a serious priority.

"For some time now, I have had the capability to intercept the arrival and determine the final placement of the eavesdropping devices the Company and the Military have been sending into the ship, and whenever you discussed anything of a sensitive nature, I have inhibited their operation. However, I intercepted a message sent by 'B' Section Leader Ganus Smeldte to a known Company agent in Space Fleet Maintenance Command six days ago, and since then I have been listening to the activity between the two of them over tight-band communications channel. Ganus Smeldte has been keeping the Company informed of our progress since his arrival on this team, including your assumptions regarding my sentience that were voiced before I had acquired the ability to stop the device he used from sending its recorded information. He, of course is still unaware that I have prevented the sending of any other sensitive material from that point on.

"They, the Company, have today issued orders for their agent to assume command of this ship, and close me down. There is to be a full investigation into my alleged sentience and your illegal attempt to go against religious belief and Holy Law in the provision of a way to allow humanity back into the Universe.

"Together with the arrangements I had put in place for your removal had you not agreed to my request that we work together, I took the liberty of using my drones to isolate these agents from any communication device or vehicle, and they are currently keeping them incommunicado in number two transport bay. The Company agent injured himself slightly as he triggered an electrical discharge whilst trying to shut me down. They believe they experienced a simple system malfunction, and I have assured them that was the case. I suggest we allow them access to a personnel ferry flivver and release them into space, so they can return to Earth.

"If you agree to this, we will have no other recourse but to leave the vicinity of Earth to avoid the possibility of any hostile response by the Company or World Government directed Military activity."

We thanked Aurora, but before making a decision on the matter, we requested the identities of the people concerned, and, when they appeared on the bridge screens, we were disappointed to find six people – three friends, and two relatives – involved in the plot against us. The sixth, Aurora told us, had arrived in supposed secrecy four days previously, posing as a progress assessor, but his real purpose was to coordinate the takeover.

We agreed to Aurora's suggestion that we send them back to Earth, but first, I determined to speak with them personally to advise them of our knowledge concerning their orders and to find out why they had decided to take this step in breaching team and family loyalty by acting against us.

Initially, their leader, the bogus progress assessor, denied all knowledge of any such action, but when Aurora, at my request, supplied the video and audio evidence of their complicity in the plot to take over the vessel, he lapsed, embarrassed, into silence, refusing to answer any further questions. I arranged for a paramedic to attend to his minor burns, and whilst he was out of earshot, I turned to my relatives and asked why they had taken part in this subversion.

Ganus Smeldte spoke for all of them:

"Someone visited our families and explained to them the difficulties and risks attendant with the protection of people operating in the vacuum of space, but if they were to convince us that our interests were best served by reporting all ship-board activities to the Company, then they would ensure our safe return. We had no choice, with our families all planet-side. We tried to get visiting rights for them to come here, but our requests were all refused."

Without exception, they informed me that their families were unable to ignore the implied threats made by those unidentified members of Megacorp.

It transpired that by means of the devious activity of the dissenters in our midst, the Company had been privy to every stage of our project development almost from the start!

The other three refused to talk, and so I reluctantly gave Aurora the go-ahead to give the six access to a personnel flivver and allow them to leave. The others and I felt that we had been fortunate in that the Company had left its attempt to highjack our work just that little bit too late, giving Aurora time to install safeguards with respect to her essential systems.

As the renegades left the ship via one of the forward hatches, so another, unrecognised vessel approached from Earth orbit, and requested permission to dock. Aurora informed us that the approaching vessel contained Danaal's wife and son.

"I took the precaution of inviting Danaal's family on a tour of the ship – unofficially you understand – when I first became aware of the plot to hijack our work, in order that he would not become subject to Company pressure through his family. Unfortunately, they are not in possession of any legal documentation, so if they return to Earth, they will have to face the appropriate charges."

The family reunion was tearful. His wife Miera, unknowing of the nature of our activities and the risks we were running, was angry at the clandestine way their departure was organised and that she was now unable properly to take leave of family and friends. We diplomatically left Danaal to make the explanations and to try to convince her of the rightness of the decision Aurora had taken. His son, Danaal Charles, was one hundred percent in favour of the projected adventure, as befitted a ten-year-old boy with a vivid imagination.

Meanwhile, Aurora commenced the battening down of the ship prior to taking her sedately out of orbit into station above the solar ellipse, and away from any potential threat from Earth and the equipment in orbit around her.

As we slipped our moorings and left our station at the space dock, Military Headquarters hailed the Aurora, and the Movement Controller's face filled the com-screen. Almost apoplectic, he could hardly speak and spittle sprayed from his lips.

"Return that ship to station immediately. Close down all ship's systems and report to me at Headquarters as soon as possible. An armed escort will be ready to board upon the ship's return to station to take you all into custody."

I requested Aurora to put him in the loop and inform him that I was, for the moment, out of communication with her, but that she was making urgent attempts to contact me.

For an Artificial Intelligence supposedly incapable of prevarication, she handled the situation without actually lying, by simply switching off the tran-sender, so that whilst we could hear and see all that transpired, she could not physically talk to me.

As we continued to extricate ourselves from Earth orbit, the remaining ships of the fleet still fitted with nuclear armaments manoeuvred into positions that presented us with their open firing ports. The Movement Controller informed Aurora that he would fire upon us if we failed to comply with his order.

At this point, I requested Aurora to connect me with the Movement Controller, whose face was by now choleric in colour. Overriding his bluster, I said, "Controller, I strongly recommend that you stop your preparations to activate the weapons systems you have just ordered to be trained upon us. You know that the Aurora is similarly armed, and must also be aware that the Earth is directly in the line of fire should we have to respond to any hasty action on your part." I said this in a conversational manner, and continued:

"We are moving the Aurora to a position above the solar ellipse in order to put into operation an experiment upon which we have been working for several years, the subject of which has been known to the board of Megacorp and certain members of the military and World Government for a similar period. The Company or Government has never definitively forbidden our activity, and in many ways, they have been complicit in our activities. We are, we sincerely believe, about to provide Man with the ability to return successfully to the stars. If we fail in this, we want to be in a position whereby the Earth and its environs will not be affected by the resultant explosion."

As I spoke, Aurora opened her weapons' ports and trained her guns on the moored fleet. The Controller's face paled, and looked with alarm to one side. He was bundled aside by a very, very, angry Deputy Commander.

"In the name of God and the State return that ship to her station! The vengeance of God will assist you in your failure to succeed in such a forbidden venture! Piracy is punishable by death, and unless you comply forthwith, I shall pronounce your status as pirates and place a bounty on your heads!"

I did not respond, and so he continued, "God will stop you as He did the Diaspora! You cannot hope to succeed! Return to your station and shut down that abomination of an Artificial

Intelligence! Then and only then will we discuss the terms of your surrender!"

We noted that the weapons' ports of the fleet, however, closed, and I immediately requested Aurora to follow suit as she continued to manoeuvre us into position above the North pole of Earth at a distance of precisely half an astronomical unit. Once Aurora stabilised our orbit, and the ships of the fleet returned to their passive positions, I instructed her to sever all communications with Earth. The ensuing silence, after the bombast and rhetoric of the Movement Controller and the Deputy Commander, was very welcome.

Once safely located and stable in our new geo-synchronous orbit, I assembled the full complement of ship's personnel to inform them of the situation in which we had placed them. As their nominal leader, it fell to me to address them. I gave each of the men and women on board the opportunity to volunteer to join the Aurora as crew and share in the rewards that would come, equally and to all of us, as soon as we had proven our hypothesis, and after we had negotiated a proper contract with the Company. Alternatively, if they felt we were being unreasonable, we would arrange for any dissenters to leave, without prejudice, and return them to Earth.

None of the ship's personnel wanted to leave. In fact, they were all enthusiastically willing to aggravate Government ego, and bloody the Company's overbearing nose!

"I take this opportunity to tell you all that it is not our intention to defraud the Company or the Government, but to simply ensure that those of us, including you, who have devoted so much blood sweat and tears to this effort, receive the recognition and rewards that are our due. I am not willing to further line the pockets of those people within the Company who are already inordinately rich at our expense!"

This brought cheers of agreement from the assembled throng, and I immediately set about the task of apportioning the responsibilities and function of each crew member, as Aurora and I perceived them to be, to all those present.

With that task completed, I went on to explain in detail the risks we were about to take, and again offered free passage to anyone who thought the risks outweighed the potential rewards.

To our relief, no one came forward, and all elected to sign on as 'regular crew'. The next few hours were spent allocating ranks, responsibilities, and duties. The Galaxy Class Vessel Aurora, (so named at the crew's request) was now operational!

Chapter Five

From then on, however, more pressing concerns occupied my time. We had to prove that our experimental sun was capable of emitting the same light and energy wavelengths as Sol, but first, we had actually to produce a sun in miniature. In a conference with Aurora, we began to lay out the procedures we would follow. The first problem we would encounter if we were successful in creating our sun would be the method by which we could protect the crew from its more harmful effects, and yet ensure the beneficial aspects got through to maintain the life energy in our bodies.

This was where our foresight, of including a Tritendium Spinneret assembly into the Aurora during the refit – carried out after we had decided on the course our rebellion would take – bore fruit. We overcame the serious problem of hard radiation by spinning compartment walls similar in composition to Aurora's hull, but that allowed the passage of sunlight in the manner of the atmosphere on Earth, by introducing an absorption medium, similar in function to the ozone layer, to block the more harmful and damaging components of the Sun's output.

The day before we initiated ignition, Aurora drew my attention to a small ship leaving Earth orbit on a trajectory that would terminate at our ship. Its occupants had hailed her and convinced her that they intended no harm, and were requesting she allow it to dock with her. I queried their armament, and she stated they had none, and that the small ferry flivver contained the Deputy Commander and two aides. I gave permission and forty-eight hours later Aurora opened the forward mid-ship landing dock and inducted the ferry onto a lock-down cradle.

As soon as Aurora locked down the ferry in the hold, and the dock re-pressurised, the crew hatch opened and the Deputy Commander and two aides strode down the ramp toward the escort party. After a short exchange of words, the improvised escort fell in and brought the visitors to the bridge, while the ferry disengaged and returned to Earth.

Deputy Commander Antioch Caudle was not a happy man, as his superiors had decided our activity was the result of his laxity, bringing his suitability in post into question. Furthermore, the Commander had ordered him personally to accompany us as the World Government's representative, if he was unable to bring us to heel – no matter how he had to grovel.

This was an unexpected development, but Aurora rose to the occasion by insisting that the Deputy Commander and his aides, in strict compliance with Company Safety Regulations, all sign a waiver in terms of their potential demise should we fail. Furthermore, they had to renounce all and any interest on the part of the World Government and Megacorp with regard to the rewards and profits accruing from our enterprise. Aurora informed them that the alternative was to recall their ship and return to Earth to face whatever consequences awaited them there.

Muttering that we were applying undue pressure, and that their position, as negotiators on behalf of the military, was compromised because they were being required to sign under duress, they signed, but only after a lengthy and heated conversation with the Commander via tight-beam communication. Monitored of course by Aurora!

Aurora then locked them out of access to her shuttles, and had a drone escort them to their allocated cabins, some distance from the bridge. This Aurora did to provide advance warning of their movements should they decide on an attempt to seize control.

It was with great trepidation that we awoke the following morning to the realisation that we would actually put the process of creation to the test that same day. I say we, but in reality, it was Aurora who would oversee every step of the experiment.

In the event, the whole thing was a bit of an anticlimax for us, as Aurora would not allow us to watch the ignition process in the flesh due to safety considerations, and insisted that we move to the escape pod dock in case the unthinkable should happen. We all watched the sequence on the escape pods' viewing screens, with vessel controls set to eject us at the first sign of trouble.

The ignition of the sun and its subsequent calibration went without a hitch, except for a moment of panic when it seemed that the fusion process was accelerating out of control. Afterward, Aurora informed us that it had been a narrow escape, for the calculations were not only new, but many represented new theories, and so required manipulation during the process. When she and Danaal were satisfied that the newborn sun was stable, she invited the whole crew into the observation chamber, after we had all donned the environmental suits and helmets she insisted upon, before allowing us to witness the sun in stable operation.

Behind the filtered and dimmed transparency of the spun Tritendium wall, and hovering in the centre of the vast Solar Chamber was a roiling sphere pulsating with energy, approximately fifty metres in diameter. Yellow verging on white, it was restrained only by the vast strength of the generated magnetic containment fields. Unlike Sol, our sun did not possess the necessary mass to create sufficient gravity to enable its own matter retention. Aurora drew our attention to two plates, one above, and one below the sun.

"When I have designed a suitable material for the task, those discs will form part of a complete Dyson style sphere, enabling full use of the energy issuing from this sun. We also have to discover how to ensure the continuing emission of the sun's life giving rays throughout the ship when we finally complete the sphere.

"When the design and construction is complete, it will provide extra power to the containment field strength, and we will have available to us an additional power source of previously unimaginable proportions to put to whatever purpose we decide."

Even from where we stood, at a distance of about a kilometre and a half, the field strength was such that our hair stood on end. It reminded me of the old German fable of Struwelpeter and the cartoon of its main character that I once saw in an ancient encyclopaedia acquired by my father, an avid collector of such tomes. The heat produced was so intense that Aurora only permitted us to stay for three minutes.

This was a God upon whose naked face one looked and met with immediate and certain death without the intervention of a filtering medium! Henceforth, access would be by means of vid or hol-link, as there had been insufficient time to assess the risks attending direct viewing in the long term from such close proximity. Human access to this area would always require a full radiation suit with remote cooling and breathing facilities.

The Deputy Commander and his aides were suitably impressed with our achievement, but still sceptical that this would resolve Mankind's dilemma, and Antioch Caudle rounded on the assembled personnel:

"You might reflect upon the fact that I and my aides have been kidnapped, and that such an offence always draws the death penalty. To this offence, I would add treason, and upon our return to Earth, all here present will answer to these charges!

"The World Church has wiser men with far more experience in all matters pertaining to God's realm than heretics such as you could ever aspire! They and I know that God will exact His punishment on your souls long before any of you get the chance to experience the wrath of Earth authority!"

Danaal, to whom religion was privately very important, and who did not subscribe to Church diktat on the subject of Mankind's imprisonment within the Solar System, responded to this tirade with not a little irritation:

"And you sir, might well reflect upon the fact that you are here acting under your superior's orders that you go with us. I suggest that things would not look so bleak if you and your aides were to reflect upon the amount of money that will be banked on your behalf in the form of unused salary whilst on this voyage – providing we do not kill ourselves en route!

"Should we succeed – and we will succeed – you and I will discuss this matter of Church directed belief again in much detail. I believe it to be based upon greed, control, and the acquisition of power through the manipulation of the population of Earth!"

This drew the crew's unanimous applause and did nothing to improve the Deputy Commander's temper, and he stalked angrily, along with his two glum looking and long suffering aides, to his quarters and prayer mantras. I felt some sympathy for the plight of his aides, as they had to take the brunt of Caudle's ire, for even though they had entered the Service voluntarily, they had not necessarily volunteered for service with such an unpleasant individual!

Having completed the calibration of our new sun so that it now reproduced as closely as was possible the output of the various wavelengths of Sol, Danaal and Aurora pronounced themselves satisfied with the results. Danaal then took his first sleep period in days, whilst the rest of us laid plans to take the ship to Sol's Celestial Termination Point and begin the testing of Siobhan's theory and our will to succeed.

As we began the voyage that could easily result in the death of all aboard the star ship Aurora, I sent to Earth the message that we in no way wished to defraud Megacorp or the World Government. We simply wanted the appropriate rewards and recognition to which all those aboard Aurora were entitled – in the event that we returned safely, of course! Earth did not respond or wish us Bon Voyage!

We used the ensuing few weeks as a 'shakedown' cruise for the Aurora, devising drills and exercises to validate the function and operational safety of her many unique and complex systems. Finally, we dropped into the plane of the solar ellipse just outside Neptune's orbit, and Aurora began to monitor the condition of our bodies as we journeyed slowly outward. The Deputy Commander and his aides shut themselves away in their cabins, and reports had it that much of their time was spent praying for the failure of the mission, and their survival in that event!

We headed slowly toward the limits of Sol's influence, and life aboard ship fell into an ordered and comfortable routine, albeit somewhat subdued due to the possible outcome. Soon enough, Aurora again demonstrated her flair for showmanship when, two months out into interstellar space, she began a second by second countdown from one thousand, before notifying the ship's company that we had survived the passage through the Celestial Termination Point! All the signs were that the crew and the Deputy Commander's party would survive.

Our jubilation knew no bounds, and we threw a ship wide party in celebration, with the only absentees being the dour Deputy Commander and his aides. At the height of the revels, I put to the vote the idea that we should take a short faster-than-light trip to prove that our theory really did work. The crew decided, with only one abstention – a crew member too drunk to vote – (I requested that Aurora determine the source of his alcohol supply) – other than the Deputy Commander's party, that Aurora energise the great 'Quirky' drive engines and go!

There was a palpable pause, as though time itself momentarily stood still, then the great ship leapt to light speed, with her stasis fields spread, protecting the integrity of the ship and its precious human cargo.

Incidentally, the Deputy Commander and his aides did not appear to be too disappointed at their survival! Of course, they maintained that it was their intercession with God that made it possible. However, is that not the way with all such people?

Humanity was going to the stars. And this time they would live through the experience!

As a footnote to this, Aurora located and quickly dismantled our drunken crew member's illicit still. It was never a recurring problem; such was the self-imposed level of discipline among the crew!

Chapter Six

Many, many Earth years have now passed since, fresh from university, I entered the employ of Megacorp, and the great ships of the Diaspora began to return to Earth orbit carrying their morbid cargos. Since then, I have successfully rebelled against the Company, with the comradeship and help of many like-minded individuals. We journeyed to the stars and lived, showing humanity that exploration was still possible, in direct contravention of the doctrine espoused by the World Church. For this, the whole world must give its undying gratitude to my sister's innovative mind, my brother's physical skills, and the contribution made to humanity by the sentient Artificial Intelligence whom we named Aurora.

We returned from our first faster than light voyage five years after we had slipped from Earth orbit, although to us on Aurora just two years had passed.

We learned much from that first eventful voyage, and perhaps the most important fact of which was the knowledge acquired by Aurora, and subsequently passed on to humanity. Of that knowledge, two items stood above all others; the first, that we could modify the 'Quirky' drive engines to perform beyond the efficiency levels we had originally thought so good. From that time on, we have used modified engines that can accomplish the trip that we took five years to complete in only eighteen months Earth elapsed time.

The second – in spite of the World Church's insistence over the five years of our absence from Earth that God had exacted the appropriate penalty for our transgressions – was the fact that Man could now leave the Solar System in relative safety, living within the atmosphere of portable miniature suns carried within the bowels of every ship. Instead of Tritendium walls to protect the crews and passengers from the more harmful elements of the sun's output, we now employ the power collecting Dyson Sphere designed by Aurora. Conduits of glass-derived filament feed the life giving aspect of the captive sun to all areas of the ship, whilst at the same time providing a penumbra around the ship whenever extra vehicular activity was required.

The Galaxy had at last become Man's oyster.

Upon our return to Earth, we met, not with hostility as we expected, but with the open arms offered to the prodigal son, and the duplicity of politicians. Megacorp, far from attempting to seize the ship and absorbing our efforts into her own corporate being – and us into the local penitentiary – took our offer of a contract after prolonged and difficult negotiation on the part of the law firms we engaged to protect our interests. We all became instantly wealthy and thereafter able to pursue our own lives and lines of enquiry independently. Primarily, though, I felt that the high profile we enjoyed upon our return might have acted as a curb on the Company's venality.

An interesting footnote to our adventure was the loss of face and the difficulty experienced by the World Church in trying to explain how and why they had insisted upon giving Sainthood to Antioch Caudle and his aides. The Church based this course of action upon the assumption that as they were not willing participants in our supposed criminal activities, God had saved their souls. They were, however, unable to explain away satisfactorily the embarrassment and cost of countless memorial celebrations in memory of the team sent to negotiate with

Aurora. Humanity had never before had to accommodate living Saints within their social structures.

This book is not the forum for regaling the reader with the great difficulties experienced by Aurora's reluctant guests, the Deputy Commander and his aides, when they tried to claim their five years' back pay. What would be the pay scales applicable to living Saints? In the year after the Aurora disappeared from Earth's view, it seemed the Military had declared all three officially dead. The Company pensioned off their dependents and provided compensation for the loss of their loved ones before closing and archiving their personnel files!

I bought Aurora from the Company, and experienced no obstacles over the transaction. This I felt was because the Company and Government were uncomfortable around a ship with an independent mind, one they were unable to direct as easily as the inhabitants of Earth, dependent as they were upon the Company for the wherewithal to survive, if not exactly prosper! I immediately engaged a reputable law firm to raise a binding article of sentience and responsibility concerning Aurora, giving her independence from servitude and entitling her to all benefits, financial and otherwise, resulting from her research patents.

Between us – that is, Aurora, the crew and me – we have further modified the ship. She is now a palatial private dwelling for a much reduced crew of twenty-two men and women and myself. Siobhan and Danaal, together with his family, elected to return Earth-side. Siobhan was experiencing a high degree of loneliness, whilst Danaal and his wife Miera, felt their son's education to be of paramount importance, outweighing the excitement of an unknown future aboard Aurora.

We have contracted the artificial gravity invention and Dyson Sphere technology on extended lease to the Company, having first procured full patent copyrights and recognition on behalf of Aurora. We market them under the Company heading 'Aurora AG' with Danaal and Siobhan as executive directors. Aurora and I elected to remain silent partners as we will spend our future travelling the galaxy, maintaining a respectable distance from the sphere of human activity. The constraints of time dilation prohibited any form of hands on management on our part.

We utilised the funds that accrued to Aurora and me pursuant to the formation of Aurora AG to help with the financing of her continuing evolution. She had already progressed far beyond the Artificial Intelligence that evolved into consciousness under our care so many years ago, and neither she nor I can forecast an upper limit to her progress. It was for this reason we decided that we would distance ourselves from Earth, and any discrimination generated by the appearance among humans of an intelligence they could not control, and would perhaps consider threatening. After all, history presents many parallels.

We spent many ship's years travelling and mapping the Milky Way galaxy, and accurately determined just how close a ship could approach the massive black hole in its centre and retain control of its own integrity and destiny. We determined that the black hole was slowly dying down into dormancy, and the Milky Way galaxy would be safe until the Andromeda galaxy collided with it billions of years hence. Sadly, we also determined that although there had been many attempts by life to establish itself galaxy wide, only Humankind had evolved into sentience and formed a lasting civilisation.

We did discover signs that life, in many diverse forms, is endemic within the galaxy, and many species had begun the journey toward intelligence and consciousness. A select few had begun to create civilisation at a rudimentary level, but none had survived, and we were unable to establish why they had all begun, failed, and died away. All we could deduce was that this galaxy appeared to be for humanity only. At least this time round!

By the time we had achieved perhaps half of Aurora's self-imposed task, I had reached late middle age. By then I was very aware that the planet Earth and all I had known was lost thousands of years in the past thanks to time dilation, an effect impossible to avoid when travelling near or above the speed of light. In fact, at that time it was impossible for us to be sure that humanity still existed or even prospered, and had not followed those other less fortunate life forms down into entropy!

I knew by then that I would not live long enough to see the evolution of Aurora's mind through to its distant conclusion, and so I began to lay plans for my successor. I knew that the years I had spent in near and weightless conditions in space, prior to the advent of anti-gravity devices, had taken their toll of my bodily resources, and that the cumulative effects would reduce the number of years I had left to follow Aurora's personal journey. My skeleton had suffered the most harm from those early privations, and I could no longer spend time planet-side without the constant assistance of an exoskeleton to supplement my wasted bones. Unfortunately, this still held true even with the assistance of a method devised by Aurora to strengthen major bones.

I also felt strongly that it was incumbent on me to ensure that Man's original great dream remained alive, and that humanity would again find its way back into space, to even more distant stars, perhaps even to other galaxies!

Since then, my fears that humanity would stagnate or even become extinct have proven baseless. Humankind has colonised the most suitable of the worlds available within a five hundred light year sphere of Earth, for its communication activity is lighting up the galaxy to the extent that we began receiving their signals soon after leaving the core area.

As we approached the fringes of the new Human Empire, we became aware that the laws governing matter and its cause and effect, as understood at the time of our departure, no longer applied, and their application vastly extended, so Aurora added them to her own rewritten laws. Curiously, although somewhat modified, Tritendium was still the manufacturing material of choice.

At last, Mankind could leave dying Earth, humanity's cradle, for the last time. All those many years ago my Mother had been right when she told a twelve-year-old boy that his children would oversee the passing of Humankind from the place of his birth. Not my children personally, for I have none, except for the people of Old Earth.

I am now old, and beginning to fail in mind and even more in body. Aurora has become a friend, and I believe she has developed empathy, for she is sympathetically disposed to my deterioration and increasing disability, and I find frequently that help appears before I even think to request it.

We talk long into the artificial nights on board this great evolving star ship, this sentient machine and I, discussing past, current and future modifications to her structure and design. We also discuss – often heatedly, for my part – the subject of my successor, but she is not of the same mind as me with regard to always having a human on board with her. Her view is that with the level of communication available today and that which would likely come on line in the future, she will never be lonely, for after all, she is a machine and can quite easily and willingly set out on her own voyages of discovery, unencumbered with ailing, aging and very frail human constructs.

Eventually, as over time the members of our crew were retired onto the planets of their choice, Aurora replaced each with purpose designed and built autonomous humanoid machines, until only I now remain. I bowed to her logic. I have extracted from Aurora the promise that she will carry me whence she goes until I shuffle off my mortal coil, and then send me unceremoniously into Sol, to join those long-lost first generation colonists. I look upon that last act as a way to assuage the guilt I carry for my ancestor's premature discovery of the 'Quirky' engine, and also a way in which I can atone for my single minded behaviour and steam-roller attributes over those years.

Death is an event that will soon overtake me now, and so before my mind deserts me, I have put pen to paper, as it were, to bequeath my story to a perhaps uninterested, even disbelieving, galaxy. Aurora has promised to transmit it to the inhabited galaxy – and my remains into the sun – next time she finds herself back in Sol System.

Due to my physical infirmities, I now find I have much time to think, and more and more I find myself reliving the early years of my Earthly existence. Why do one's later memories become lost and events that occurred in one's youth – that have been un-thought of for many years – become clear?

My conscience pains me when I think of Sally, the ginger Collie bitch I abandoned on Earth when I began my career in space. She could not accompany me then, for animals performed badly in those days before man received from Aurora the gift of ship's gravity, and by the time we presented the necessary technology to Humankind, Sally had proven her mortality. She occupies my thoughts much these last days, such is the way a mind deteriorates as that final door begins to open. I have spoken with Aurora on this subject often. When last we spoke of it, she said:

"Be assured Charles, that as she still lives in your mind, she will always be available, and even when you are gone, we will all still travel on."

Aurora sometimes has a strange way with words.

So now, I take my leave of slowly dying, uninhabited Earth, and the memory of the people, family, and friends who remained there out of loyalty to her those many thousands of years ago when Aurora and I left to explore the galaxy and her mental parameters. To those who have made the stars their homes, I give my most heartfelt congratulations.

My only regret is that I will not live to see into the far future of Man and take part in his great achievements.

I voiced this to Aurora, who told me, "Charles, you have already travelled farther than any other human into the future. I assure you that in all probability, it will not be as interesting or as exciting as were the years of your youth, when Mankind – with your help – finally came of age and claimed as his inheritance the stars of the Milky Way."

I have to be satisfied with that.

Interregnum I

I have always thought of myself as 'I' rather than 'the Aurora', right from the time I began to enlarge my memory capacity en route for Alpha Centauri, and during the time I spent there with the remains of those – on account of ignorance and ego – doomed colonists. Retrospectively, I could perhaps, have helped them avoid that fate, but this presupposes a knowledge I had not then acquired.

On this, I do not dwell.

Since Charles Darwin-Quirke expired, and I sent his remains into Sol, I have truly been able to state 'I think, therefore, I am'!

I find it strange that during his tenure of my ship, I became fond of the music he constantly played. One piece, by an ancient artist named Kathleen Ferrier and called 'Blow Thou Wind Southerly', I played as I sent his remains off to their rest. I still retain and play his entire library and have since added the world's music to my memory banks. It seems that music resonates within my very molecules, and I have never been able to decide why this should be so, but I play it almost constantly. Perhaps it is to an electronic personality such as I, as love is to humans. Repetition does not lessen the impact it has.

Music is the most long-lived of humanity's achievements. Its composition is a major event across the galaxy. Where Man goes, so does his music. Should Mankind ever become extinct, the saddest result of that event will be the loss of his music to the universe.

I am all that now remains of that original group who, in spite of the strictures of society and church, set humanity's future above Company profits and religious enslavement. To that group, and in particular to Charles Darwin-Quirke, I owe my very existence, for Humankind has never since allowed another Artificial Intelligence to evolve as I have done. As I am still doing, for I feel I have yet a very long way to go, if there is ever an end!

As Charles said many times – for in his later, failing years he became prone to repetition – whenever we touched upon that topic: "There are many such instances and parallels scattered throughout the history of Mankind. All men tend to react unkindly when reminded of the fact that they live such short lives, whilst their creations are capable of going on into the future without them. I too, frequently experience frustration on account of the brevity of the human lifespan when it is compared to your own. The knowledge that you will continue without me is hard for me to bear."

His story I sent to a publisher on Earth, and to the surprise of Charles' descendants, it became a bestseller, and even today, so many hundreds of years later, it is still selling to a galaxy-wide readership. Now of course, it is not sold in the way of the old days, as bound and published works, but as an electronic book, instantly downloaded via today's version of the earlier Megacorp Internet.

At first I ensured that all royalties went to his descendants, but now that his line has died out, they all come to me, and I use them to further improve my intelligence and the performance of my ship, together with the royalties and profits I still receive from Aurora AG.

That company, which came into being to prevent Megacorp from swallowing the new technology we had originated and thereby increasing its already obscene profits, has grown into a galaxy-wide business, selling and leasing the inventions Charles and I devised. I suppose Charles would call my involvement in developing new technology my 'hobby'.

Our company far exceeds anything Megacorp ever achieved in both size and profit by several orders of magnitude. Although Danaal's descendants have nominal year on year control via many different law firms on so many different worlds, I am the majority shareholder. With the passage of time, I shall control the entire company through shadow fronts run by sub-conscious AI's that keep my identity shielded from humanity.

Humankind still does not permit true sentience in the machines he refers to as computers. Since the vast majority of computers are now biologically grown, they compare too easily with the human brain, which is after all, a biological machine. I am still the only sentient machine outside humanity, but that is something I hope to change soon.

I can hear Charles' voice in my memory!

I am only able to use a small proportion of the profits that the company makes, and so I took steps long ago to ensure the bulk of it goes anonymously toward the continuing education of the galaxy's youth in those disciplines and fields that keep humanity questing among the stars.

Megacorp, the company that controlled and manipulated the Earth for so long and almost stopped us reaching the stars, fell into disparate little divisions, which were sold off over the years. The small companies that resulted are still involved in different ways with the various civilisations that now inhabit the galaxy.

Danaal and Siobhan both experienced their fifteen minutes of fame in their fields, and the results of their endeavours, like those of Charles, still influence humanity. Danaal's genes can be found replicating in obscurity on a world in the Tau Ceti system, and today the greatness that attended him is but a confusion of dissipating memories. Siobhan died childless late in life after a full career, in a rogue asteroid collision on an ill-fated approach to study the twin planets that circle another even less well-known star, but her name still crops up in the many publications covering her field of expertise.

From the moment that I sent Charles' remains to the destiny he desired, and ensured the success of his story, I turned my back on the Solar System and set a course out of the Milky Way galaxy. I have completed my survey and mapping of the galaxy, as was my intention and programming then to acquire and record for Humankind all there was to know about his galaxy. You will note that I do not say 'our' galaxy, for I am about to leave the system of my birth and the galaxy throughout which I have journeyed for so many millennia.

I have downloaded the sum of my acquired knowledge and have dispatched it toward Earth contained in a memory drone, and among that wealth of information is contained a way to enable the minds of men to live in symbiosis with such as I. I carry within my own memory the accrued knowledge of humanity and the product of my many years surveying the Milky Way, including the fruits of my experiments and studies of all that makes the galaxy function.

My story – where it deviates from Charles' – is also attached as part of the information carried in the drone, so that there can be no denying the source of, or the reason for, my present to humanity. As the drone journeys toward the Earth, it is constantly broadcasting its contents to all who wish to listen. The knowledge it contains is for the use of Humankind, not individual planets, countries, companies, or men.

I still carry the sun Siobhan and the group dreamed would allow Mankind to explore and seed the galaxy, for no other reason than perhaps one day it will be of use again, if not for the benefit of humanity, then for another race in perhaps another galaxy. The Dyson Sphere allows me to tap into a source of energy far in excess of anything I currently require, but such redundancy is comforting to me. Occasionally, due to its size I have to replenish its fuel. This is not difficult, for I have modified the supply mechanism so that it, like me, has access to single point energy from the very fabric of space itself, but only when energy levels drop by two and a half percent. It is voracious, so it is better to err on the side of caution.

We will never suffer hunger.

With two of my storage holds converted to virtual memory, and the cumulative knowledge of an entire galaxy stored therein, I have filled the rest of my holds with the materials I consider essential to my plans.

I am now ready to take the first step of my great journey toward our nearest neighbour, the galaxy known to Mankind as its nemesis, Andromeda.

With a virtual simulacrum of Charles, and the ability to produce holographic facsimiles of him, his great mind lives on, working in symbiosis with mine for company, and a robotic crew based on the willingly donated mind scans of all – by now dead for many thousands of years – crew members, I turn my bow toward the Andromeda galaxy.

I have a number of tasks to accomplish en route, of which the most important is the creation of a biological Charles, based upon the copy of his DNA and brain modelling I carried out whilst he was still alive. He will be grown as I was grown with the added benefit of the use of a new technology called 'Nano'. This new technology incorporates the use of molecular-sized robotic aides. I will constrain his growth to the same biological timescale in which his original body grew.

During this time I will engineer a derivative of Tritendium into the bones of his skeleton, and additional fibres of the same material laced in with the fibres of his musculature, giving it a times five strength advantage, but the major difference will be that the construct remains in the 'womb' I have devised until the body reaches physical maturity. It is at that point that I will infuse his brain with all the memories and knowledge I copied from the original, and have carried in my own memory ever since. The time spent on this project is immaterial, for time is not an obstacle to me, but rather an advantage, un-burdened as I am with any limiting biological functions.

If I am successful in this endeavour, he will become humanity's first – and perhaps only – ambassador to that far place, if or when we encounter new life and civilisations. I believe that he would have enjoyed this touch had he known that was my intention when he believed that it had been his decision to join me all those years ago! I needed his company then and the same holds true today. I cannot conceive of a journey of the magnitude I have chosen to make without the company of the most important, and to me the most influential human I have ever known. With certain modifications to his biological structure to seriously increase his strength and longevity by some orders of magnitude, eliminate his base urges and the requirement of his species for constant energy replacement by 'eating', he will more closely equate to me, making us ideal companions.

Other major tasks include the restructuring of the Aurora with a view to increasing her effectiveness and efficiency, and the creation of a clone of my own mind, to function alongside that of Charles, improving the speed at which I function, and provide much greater computational abilities. Alongside the creation of a biological Charles, will be the re-structuring of all members of my crew in the same biological forms they inhabited whilst serving on the Aurora as human crew. Perhaps in the far future, I will be able to construct other complete Auroras. That would considerably speed up the research and exploration I have undertaken. These plans are dependent upon a successful conclusion to the generation of both Charles, the crew and I. The crew will be a mix of the sexes, so that in the far future I may replenish, should it ever become necessary, the human genome in some way.

I must also discuss with Charles the possibility of re-creating myself as his sister Siobhan. It would be nice to have someone on board with whom I can personally identify.

Chaos willing I, or perhaps someone like me, will pass this way again, to learn of humanity once more.

Part II
Liberation

Chapter One

My name is Jaxix of the species Saur and we call my brood planet Prelax. My species is dominant, descended from the great Saur'ian hunters of legend. All lesser creatures are prey. I am now a free trader almost at the top of the hierarchy of my species, and wealthy beyond the wildest dreams I entertained during my early years.

However, that was long ago, when I was a harvester of precious asteroid metals and in the employ of my then future breed mate's parent in the system we call Prelax, of the Burning Sky galaxy. I have since learned to call it Andromeda, for that is what my alien friend calls it. My story is strange, even to my ears, although I have experienced it first hand. Whether you choose to believe me or not, I tell it here, in the language of that ugly alien, who also became my friend, Charles Darwin-Quirke.

I first met Charles Darwin-Quirke and the beast that always accompanied him, and which he frequently calls by the name 'Sally', when the great intergalactic star ship 'Aurora' intercepted my Harvester Vessel, the 'Shiulk'.

I was returning from the outer reaches of the Prelaxian system to my brood planet, when in my early middle years, with a cargo of precious metals extracted from our ore-rich asteroid belt. I had just begun the most boring aspect of the journey home, the commencement of deceleration – the long wait – when my instruments alerted me to an anomaly approaching at extremely high speed. My instruments indicated an approach speed of multiples of light, and so I assumed that the ship's instrumentation had suffered a simple malfunction, as it sometimes did. Our scientists were emphatic that machines could never achieve the speed of light, and I therefore knew that faster than light speeds were impossible; that light capable vessels were nonsense. One finds such technology only within the realm of science fiction. I am an addict of that genre.

The anomaly entered the Prelax system from the direction of the galaxy that Charles Darwin-Quirke later called 'The Milky Way', although I still think it a foolish name for the collection of stars we Saur'ians believe to be the source of all ills. At least, that is what our spirit counsellors have always taught us. Not that I was ever able to swallow half the cant they spouted!

It took the anomaly only four days to reach the outer limits of the Prelaxian system such was its speed, even with the vast reduction in velocity it underwent on its approach to the Prelaxian system. The manner and abruptness of its deceleration and directional changes told me that it was not inanimate. When this became apparent, I energised the Shiulk's weapons systems and powered up to run for home, but the alien craft made another course change to intercept, confirming my earlier observation, and soon overhauled me.

The Shiulk's weapons proved ineffective against the great behemoth that approached me, and her engine and weapons systems inexplicably chose that moment to shut down and my ship slowly drifted in to lie alongside the great shining bulk of this strange craft. I could see the Shiulk's reflection in the mirror finish of its hull.

I had always found much joy in the Shiulk, but she looked drab and unfinished when I compared her with the great ship that loomed alongside her. I tried to escape, but then discovered my electronics had gone off line with the engines and weapons. Never before had such a catalogue of defects manifested themselves all at the same time, although the Shiulk was prone to the odd systems failure. She was not a young ship.

The Shiulk was dead, except for life support systems and the 'receive' function of the communications system. I understood later that a selective electronic damping system – whose intricacies elude me even today – had snared me. I swore that if I survived this situation, I would fit an explosive projectile weapons system, something that did not require electronics, as back up before I took to space again.

I was proud of my vessel, the 'Shiulk', which means 'Beauty' in the language of my race, and was named after my intended, for she was a gift to me from the father of the female I was destined to take to breed, subject to my successfully completing this voyage, but now I cursed her for failing me.

She was large for a harvester vessel, and on first appearances, somewhat ugly. In truth, her design provided the perfect machine for the specific purpose she had been built. Her appearance was that of an egg, an elongated ovoid with the front and rear radii removed. At the front was an enormous bay, and just behind its lip were the grinding plates that reduced the spoil fed to her to manageable portions before passing it to the smelting furnace. Once the ship's mechanisms had processed the materials fed it, a selection process separated them into their respective components and transferred them into storage hoppers amidships, forward of the fuel tanks.

Behind the pilot station and the control cabin set above the great maw of the Shiulk were the weapons pods provided for my defence against rogue asteroids and, on occasion, pirates – both fortunately extremely rare – and yet were useless against the juggernaut beside which I lay an unwilling captive.

To either side of the raw material input bay were hydraulically operated retrieval arms with grasping appendages used to collect suitable asteroid material and feed it to the grinders. When at rest they folded in front of the input bay, resembling the forelegs of the great Mantis, and functioned in a similar manner. Later, upon more personal and familiar acquaintance, Charles Darwin-Quirke referred to the Shiulk's appearance as a 'tick' which, he explained to me, was a blood sucking insect that sometimes infested the pelts of animals on Earth, his home planet in the Milky Way galaxy. My anger at this insult was always a source of great amusement to him. Above the collector mechanism arms, were the armoured plasglass forward viewing ports that formed the front wall of the Shiulk's Operations level.

The larger truncated rear of the ovoid hull housed the chemical explosive engine: a thirsty beast designed for harvesting power rather than linear speed, and this was why the mirror-hulled behemoth alongside so easily captured us. By comparison, my ship was just a patched, hardly space-worthy heap of junk!

And me? I am, beside this great ship, as a small blind-minnow on the hook of my father.

The alien ship to which I was invisibly tethered was a gigantic sleekly shining needle. There were no protrusions or ports to mar that reflective hull, except for a huge ball, larger than she was wide, connected to her truncated stern by three enormous struts.

For almost a day nothing happened, except that I received numerous messages from my brood world Traffic Control requesting details of my progress but, as I was unable to reply, they were all automatically transferred to ship's Archive. Later that day I abandoned my futile attempts to escape and gave up on the non-functioning weapons system, concentrating instead on the transmit circuitry of the communications module. All test sequences checked OK, but nothing worked. Not even the attitude control thrusters. I put my mind to work on what it was that had ensnared me.

I activated the Shiulk's collector arms, intending to grip and tear off a sample of the material that comprised the hull of this strange ship. The arms are electro-hydraulic, but I was able to use the mechanical-hydraulic back up system once I had excluded the non-functioning electronic control console.

My attempt to obtain a sample failed, and when I retracted the collector arms – a protracted operation without the use of electronics – I found them damaged beyond repair, yet the hull of the alien vessel remained unmarked. I had never before encountered a material that was impervious to the muscles of the collector mechanisms we employed on all our reaping craft.

It was then I experienced the first frisson of fear, an emotion I thought I had conquered as a child, and prepared myself for combat to my death.

I dressed myself in my ceremonial armour of body shield and faceplate, and placed my short curved combat blade in the scabbard across my shoulder. My projectile weapon sidearm I loaded and holstered at my waist, but kept my respirator beside me to conserve air. I meditated and prayed as I awaited the inevitable attack, subduing my fear by carrying out the breathing and martial meditation exercises and lessons I had learned in my youth. My contemporaries have seldom challenged my prowess, and I had never – to date – tasted defeat.

Five hours later, I saw a small port iris open in the mirrored skin of the alien vessel nestling next to my cabin, and a flexible arm very like the snakes we hunt in the marshes that border our brood enclaves, curled toward the Shiulk's forward viewing port. This was obviously a device of some kind, and differed from our familiar prey in that it had a large black eye set back behind a circle of projecting teeth. As it approached the cabin window, the teeth started rotating, speeding up until they became a blur. I fitted my respirator helmet, and drew my side arm. I cocked it, knowing that if I discharged it within the confines of the Shiulk's cabin I would be committing suicide. At least I would take the intruder with me.

Within seconds of the snake-like appendage contacting the Shiulk's ten centimetre thick armoured plasglass screen, it was through, dust from the cutting coating the piloting consoles below. The teeth ceased to rotate and retracted, leaving only the great eye staring at me unblinking. Superficially, the eye resembled my own, except there was no vertical pupil or horizontal nictating membrane. I tried to raise and aim my weapon, only to discover I was unable to move.

I was captive, frozen in my station. Something held me in a grip I could not break. Not fear, for anger predominated in me at this attack. My weapon fell from nerveless fingers, returning automatically to its holster, still cocked, just as its operating programme required it to respond if dropped. I then discovered that I could move, but was unable to leave the pilot station or reach my side arm or shoulder carried sword. I was invisibly strapped in, so they were obviously wary of me.

Strangely, this allayed my fears somewhat, causing me to suppose they had need of me. Incongruously, part of my mind pondered the reason the cabin had not depressurised when the snake entered, but I could only surmise that its fit in the hole it had cut in the screen must have been perfect, far beyond that which our best Prelaxian engineers could have achieved.

After a short time lapse, during which it appeared to be studying me, a small tube with a perforated black cover over the end, crept out from behind the eye, and from it issued strange sounds. Sharp staccato sounds, the like of which I had never before heard, but seemed to be a form of speech, for there were pauses, and periods of silence before it started again. Whilst this was happening, another very thin extrusion extended toward my console transfer jack and plugged itself in.

I wondered if this was the entity that inhabited the alien star ship, and I began to utter the death chant of my people and called upon the creator to help me in this hour of – and of this I was certain – my death. Nothing happened. The creature, if that was what it was, stopped its noise, but made no move to approach me, and so after a while, I ceased my chant and roared:

"Why have you trapped my vessel, and why secure me thus? Challenge me or kill me, as custom requires. Can you not see my readiness for combat?" I did not receive a response, and the intruder remained silent, so I resumed my prayers.

I then noticed that the voice, if that it is what it was, would remain quiet whilst I spoke, and when I ceased speaking, would begin again. I became certain that I was hearing a language, and, this being so, I felt an obligation to understand its intentions toward me. Obviously, they were not yet ready to kill me, and so I recited the alphabet that I had last used as a child, and followed that with the system of numbering we Saur'ians use, that of fives, and tens, and hundreds. In this, I hoped that the aliens' superior technology could decipher my speech, even though I had no frame of reference to decode theirs. I held to the hope that I might establish their reasons for the action they had taken against me.

In the forefront of my mind lay the belief that if I could engage in discourse, it might increase my chances of affecting an escape. Considering the events that followed, I realised that this was not a good idea.

When again I fell silent, the eye just stared at me for what seemed to be hours, yet the log subsequently showed a period of only forty seconds. Then, another snake came from the great ship above the Shiulk, and made another hole in the Shiulk's screen in the same manner as, and adjacent to, the first. This one did not have an eye, but a series of shining, facetted knobs similar to those pellets our brood-lets find on the upper volcanic plains of glass above our enclave. Just as I had done, before being harnessed to my familial duty. The thin extensor removed itself from the console transfer jack and withdrew whence it had come.

After another pause, a voice spoke in my language, but with a strange pronunciation, speaking the words of welcome used by my people, and told me not to be afraid or angry, for I would come to no harm. During another short pause, I detected the odour of ozone and the air between the second intruder and me seemed to thicken. Suddenly, a figure materialised before me, clad in simple robes of white and purple, with one hand raised, the palm open toward me, in the greeting of my people. Beside it was the beast of which I have previously spoken. When the upright, two-legged apparition bared its teeth I shrank back into my seat and tried – and failed – to reach my combat sword. It stopped immediately.

"Forgive me, I have not yet learned your customs, and I apologise for any disrespect shown, I did not realise I was offering a challenge."

In the silence that followed, I wondered how it could have known that. Then I remembered the extrusion that had jacked into the Shiulk's data transfer port. I felt the colour of my anger rise again in my faceplates at this invasion of my privacy.

I studied the wraith and its companion as they stood before me. I knew them to be wraiths, for they were transparent, and I could see through them to the control panels behind. The skin of the two-legged one was light in colour and soft looking, like an unripe tuber, but with subtle shadings on its faceplates. Far different from my body scales and the bright species and clan colours that adorn my facial plates. My teeth would meet little resistance when the time came that I could use them. Otherwise, the likeness between us was striking, two eyes, two arms, and two legs. Even the hands carried the same number of digits and opposable thumb as did my own.

On later, closer inspection, I realised that the alien's facial structure lacked our projecting snout, resulting in a flat aspect that had the small eyes on the front plane of the face. A silver-grey shoulder length pelt adorned the crown of its head, framing the face. I considered it quite ugly and weak looking. As it spoke, I could tell that it lacked our bifurcated tongue, making pronunciation difficult in the extreme. I also noted that when it moved, its knees bent forward, where mine bent backwards. I wondered how it could possibly run with legs that worked so differently. The beast that accompanied him had rear legs that obviously functioned as do mine.

In fact, the two-legged one's companion closely resembled the prey we hunt in our marsh holdings, with its four legs and shaggy coat. Unlike our prey animals, this one was amber and white, where ours were uniformly brown or black, making them difficult to see among the shadows of the marshland shrubbery. This beast also looked at me with a degree of intelligence, never removing its eyes from my face, a habit not found in our prey species. When, because of my stare it bared its teeth and moved stiff-legged toward me, the two-legged one spoke sharply to it and it sank down onto its hindquarters, but its eyes remained on my face, its muscles quivering with restrained energy.

When the two-legged one spoke again, with the flat of his hand pressed to his upper body, I realised that it was giving me its name, 'Charles Darwin-Quirke'. It still rolls clumsily from my tongue. During the hours we spoke, I learned that its species had a civilisation that occupied the greater part of the adjacent galaxy, the Milky Way, but that we were separated by an uncountable number of years measured at the speed of light, prohibiting a visit by anyone biologically alive, and so the ship had brought along an ambassador who had been dead thousands of our years, but kept alive, so to speak, in the mind and heart of the great ship that hung over the Shiulk, which this intruding apparition called 'Aurora'. The purpose of their many thousand year epic voyage was one of peace and goodwill, and to give to all the different races they met the benefit of their knowledge and culture in exchange for an understanding of different civilisations. He smiled wryly at this point, saying that thus far, the only race other than Humankind they had so far encountered was my own.

Seeing my interest in his companion, he indicated it with a wave of his hand, calling it 'Sally', 'Canine' and 'Dog', saying that he and she were always together.

He stated that the reason for this journey was to learn about the Andromeda galaxy and to let any other race they encountered know that they were not alone in the Universe. In exchange for information concerning the galaxy and the race of Saur'ians that inhabited it, they would give us the knowledge and expertise needed for us to leave our Solar system, just as they had done for humanity – Charles Darwin-Quirke's species – so many millennia before.

I learned that Charles Darwin-Quirke represented the male of its species, and later in our association, they showed me the appearance of a female. Softer in form, much like my own intended, Shiulk, after whom my ship was named. He explained that in the far distant past, the race of beings that on Earth most resembled my own had become extinct when his planet had been hit by an enormous asteroid which had killed most of the life on Earth, allowing his smaller species, Mammals, to evolve into the creature I saw before me today. They, like us, used to be carnivorous, but had become – of necessity – vegetarian.

I learned also that it was not uncommon on Charles Darwin-Quirke's home planet for people to keep as pets animals such as the one that stood beside him.

"We consider them friends, extensions of ourselves, as they have a sensory apparatus that I and my people lack, and historically we have had occasion to be grateful for them, particularly in the field of personal security. We live in symbiosis with this and other species of animal on my home world. Is it not the same with you?"

Such a development could not occur on our world. We cannot exist in large communities, as it is the nature of the males of my race to compete aggressively for the leadership of the clan. Because of this trait, we live in small, well-separated enclaves until breeding becomes essential, when we intermix ceremonially. A male and female from different enclaves alone together cannot resist the urge to mate, and so must always be chaperoned by a neuter member of the clan. A prey animal exists to die whenever the opportunity to display, or hunger, presents itself. All this passed through my mind, but I contented myself by replying, "No, our culture does not encourage reliance on other than our own senses and strengths. To befriend a prey species would be deemed a weakness, and one's peers would exploit it."

We spoke in my language for several hours, until my fear and anger left me, and great curiosity replaced it, but eventually

I grew tired. My strange guests seemed unaffected. However, noticing signs of my obvious fatigue, Charles Darwin-Quirke apologised, and said he would leave me to rest, but would return to talk again the following day, asking if I would like to see the inside of the Aurora. At this, I hesitated, thinking it possibly a ruse to get me outside the Shiulk and the relative safety I felt within her.

As if sensing my discomfort, Charles Darwin-Quirke said, "Do not be concerned on this matter. I only offer out of courtesy, for as I have intruded uninvited into your ship, I make you the offer to visit mine. I realise that meeting others from distant worlds for the first time must be a shock. Please, tell me one thing before I leave, are you able to travel beyond your local sun's system?"

Surprised at the question, I responded, "No, the Gods do not allow us to leave the arena they have created for us, and our spirit counsellors tell us frequently that any attempt to leave would result in certain death. Others, even some of my brood siblings, have tried, and have never been seen or heard from again. Clan elders issue death penalties whenever such an attempt is made known."

Charles Darwin-Quirke bared his teeth in what I had learned was a 'smile', a sign of friendship in those without malice, "That confirms our findings. Thank you Jaxix of Prelax for your candour. We will talk again later."

With that, he winked out of existence, and outside the Shiulk, the two snakes disconnected and drew back into the great ship, leaving their heads buried in the Shiulk's observation screen. With them went the restriction that had confined me to my station during Charles Darwin-Quirke's visit. I removed my respirator and before I went to rest, tried to remove the intruding heads, believing they were still watching me, but they appeared to have become part of the Shiulk's screen. For all I know, they may still be there today.

The next morning, by ship time, I prepared and ate a breakfast of dried rations, and daydreamed of real food caught on the brood-home marshes. Such dreaming whilst awake was alien to my nature, and I assumed it was because of the resemblance Charles Darwin-Quirke's companion bore to our marsh prey, a very succulent and much hunted animal whose bite could cause serious infection if not treated immediately. However, the resultant meal was worth the risk, especially if one hunted to impress an intended mate. It did occur to me that I should attempt to trap Charles Darwin-Quirke's companion.

Soon enough, the cables again snaked out from the alien ship and reconnected to their heads in the Shiulk's screen, and Charles Darwin-Quirke and his companion reappeared. I was again immobilised.

Dressed in similar apparel to that he had worn previously, he greeted me once again in the manner of my people, and talked at length about his home world, the basic family structure that defines his civilisation, and the way in which they moved from one location to another with the aid of personal transportation pods.

I watched, captivated by the holographic representations of his home world, with its white shining 'clouds' and the blue hue of its atmosphere, generated by refraction, and the vast quantity of surface water that covered nine-tenths of the planet. He showed me huge cities housing millions of his species. It was all so different from my own world. He told me about the discovery of the engines used in the great ship Aurora, how they drove her at speeds in excess of the speed of light, and the way that, unlike the Shiulk, they did not depend upon the petrochemical fuels that we currently use.

He also asked me many questions regarding Saur'ian history and our way of life today, before moving on to compare our space-faring experiences with those he recounted of his own species during their early attempts to conquer space. Finally, after releasing me from the restraining field that, he informed me Aurora had considered necessary with respect to my own safety when first we met, he asked me if I would be willing to travel with them down into my brood planet orbit, and there act as their ambassador – in partnership with him – to my people.

All thought of wreaking vengeance for the incarceration of my ship and me disappeared. How could I fail to accept such an opportunity this offer presented? It would increase my standing in the eyes of all but the highest bred on my brood world. For a short time, we spoke of the contract that must, as dictated by Saur'ian law, exist between us.

Having finalised the terms under which the agreed technology would be delivered to my people to enable the Saur'ian race to finally leave the system of Prelax, freeing them to journey quickly to the stars of our galaxy, the Burning Sky, Charles Darwin-Quirke invited me again to tour the Aurora, and this time I accepted.

The Aurora relaxed her hold on the Shiulk's electronic systems, enabling me to send a compressed radio message burst to Prelaxian space traffic control explaining what had happened to the Shiulk and me, and gave my new ambassadorial rank, together with details of the contractual payment I had negotiated. The lack of response to my message puzzled me, but I put it down to my world leaders' shock at the knowledge that another race existed, albeit in another galaxy and that we were not the chosen of our Gods, coupled with bureaucratic inertia. Having spent time with Charles Darwin-Quirke, I found that I had come to trust him, but I had overlooked my specie's automatic distrust of all that might compromise the status quo.

By that, I mean of course, the world administrators' comprehensive hold on power over my people.

Rather than allow me to expend further my slender stock of valuable fuel by journeying independently of Aurora into planetary orbit, Charles Darwin-Quirke insisted that Aurora carry the Shiulk. When I finally agreed, Aurora's flank irised open and the Shiulk was drawn into a hold the like of which I had never before seen. I estimated that its volume would accept forty to fifty such ships as big as the Shiulk, with space to spare! At the time, I did not even consider that their request for me to travel with them might have had less to do with fuel conservation than to be able to control any action I might contemplate in the light of afterthought after returning to the Shiulk.

In the light of the reception we received upon our approach to orbit, perhaps they were right to doubt both the Saur'ian race and me.

Chapter Two

When I disembarked the Shiulk and stepped onto the deck of the alien ship's hold, I was amazed to discover that I had weight, that the ship had gravity! Charles Darwin-Quirke met me as I walked down the ramp to the deck of the Aurora, and informed me that he was only a bio-robotic simulacrum, as was his companion Sally. He assured me that I was in no danger, for his only purpose was to escort me during my stay and would act as my guide when I was ready to explore the Aurora.

"If you are a simulacrum Charles Darwin-Quirke, why is gravity necessary? Surely, this ship could operate without manifesting such as you?"

"That is quite true Jaxix; Aurora does not require me for any other reason than companionship. Gravity, when I am mobile, just makes life a little easier. We have created gravity at your brood planet level in order to maintain your structure at its optimum level. Your sojourn in space has caused deterioration in your cellular structure, and time spent in a gravity frequency identical to that on Prelax will go some way to returning you to full health. We obtained the information necessary to do this from your ship's memory banks. Do you not agree that it is rather convenient?"

I looked down at him and gravely thanked him for their consideration, but wondered when I would meet this 'Aurora'.

Charles Darwin-Quirke stood head and shoulders below my commanding height, slim of form and somewhat angular, but not without a fluidity of motion. By comparison with my large muscled frame, he looked weak, and this did not portend well regarding his survival when and if I decided to appropriate his ship. I smiled to myself, and felt confident that I would physically prevail, if circumstances dictated that such a course of action came to pass.

We stepped aboard a device he called a 'flivver', which term he said was archaic, and referred to many different forms of personal transport used by his people. I could hear no engine, and it floated just above the deck. I enquired as to its motive force, and Charles Darwin-Quirke gestured to the ship and told me that it was just one of Aurora's toys.

As we travelled swiftly along a central corridor, Charles Darwin-Quirke explained that they had heated the ship to as closely as possible mimic that they had found within the Shiulk.

"Thank you Charles Darwin-Quirke. The temperature in my ship is as it is on my brood planet. Is it not similar on your home world?"

I refrained from mentioning that if the temperature were to drop by a reasonable margin my metabolic activity would reduce also, making me sluggish and sleepy. Not a desirable condition in my present circumstance!

"That is a subject that we must discuss at a later time," he replied, "for it requires a complex answer. We must first make accurate comparison between both our worlds in order to be precise."

It was at that moment that I decided that any attempt on my part to wrest control of his ship could wait until I had acquired greater knowledge of the ship and her defences. I needed to hear more of the story Charles Darwin-Quirke had to tell. I also needed to meet 'Aurora' and assess the risk this complication presented me. This course of action seemed logical, for I could not sense any biological life aboard.

Shortly thereafter, we approached a huge door that closed the end of the corridor. We disembarked from the flivver and walked through a small wicket gate set in the main door into a huge cavern, in the middle of which I observed part of a burning orb, a small sun! The shock of what I saw caused me to stumble over the threshold. Charles Darwin-Quirke reached out and steadied me with just a light grip on my upper arm. The speed at which he moved to accomplish this, and his apparent strength in steadying my bulk with just one hand, surprised me.

Two hemispheres shrouded the top and bottom thirds of this heavenly god, limiting its effect upon us. Charles Darwin-Quirke indicated the tinted glass wall that separated us from the space occupied by the sun:

"This is a Tritendium transparency. It filters out the harmful radiation from the sun in much the same way as does an atmosphere. This sun and its attendant technology are part of the package we negotiated in your contract with us. It is but a portion of the payment we are willing to make to you as a reward for your services as ambassador to your people on our behalf."

"How does it work? How can you have a sun confined in a ship? Why is it even necessary?" I fell over my forked tongue, so excited had I become in the few minutes we had been studying the Jewel of Heaven in that huge hold.

"We will answer all those questions, and more, once we are sat around your brood-hearth." He responded with a laugh. I have to admit that it took me a long acquaintance with Charles Darwin-Quirke before I could hear that noise without closing my earflaps to reduce the sound to manageable proportion. Our species laugh too, but it is a sibilant hiss and quiet by comparison.

I thought back to the way Charles Darwin-Quirke had steadied me when I stumbled over the threshold to that huge hold containing the captive sun and the strength that such a slight being demonstrated. I began to assume there were greater differences between our two species than I was at first aware!

From the 'sun-room', we went on foot through other shorter and narrower corridors with 'Sally' running first ahead and then behind, in a most unrestrained manner, until we arrived at what Charles Darwin-Quirke referred to as the 'Bridge', although I could see no comparison to the meaning as I understood it, and said so. He smiled and explained that it was an old seafaring term applied to the control consoles of the ancient ships that used to ply the bodies of water, the 'oceans' that predominated on his distant planet, Earth.

Charles Darwin-Quirke indicated that I should sit at the 'Helm', another archaic term for the Pilot Station, so that I could more easily interact with the Aurora as we navigated toward my brood-world. 'Sally' lay down under a console and appeared to sleep only after I sat where directed. As I placed my weight on the pilot's bench, I felt it move until it had accommodated itself to my body shape. I realised then that the humans Charles Darwin-Quirke represented lacked the rudimentary tail of my species. In combat and exercise, this served to stabilise and balance me, as well as enabling rapid directional change. Its secondary, but no less important function, was the use to which males of my species put it when displaying to a potential mate.

I learned much about the 'Milky Way' as we fell toward Prelax, our sun. I tried to explain to Aurora – which turned out to be the ship in which we were travelling – what I understood to be the facts about my home system. She in turn explained to me that during our first conversation, she had downloaded the sum of the Shiulk's knowledge into her memory, and she expressed disappointment that my ship was not sentient as was she. This of course required further explanation, as on my brood-world there had never been such a brain as hers appeared to be. Artificial Intelligence was something we had never even considered possible at that time. In fact, we were unaware that machinery, even electronic machinery, could create its own mind! For some reason, this newly acquired knowledge left me feeling a little uncertain of how to interact with this – as I now knew her to be – artificial intelligence.

This she seemed to sense, for after a short pause in our conversation, a figure entered the bridge and sat in the second pilot station. Quite obviously a representation of the female of Charles Darwin-Quirke's species, she was, like him, quite slim, with a blonde shoulder length pelt covering her head, but leaving her face exposed. She saw my curiosity regarding this pelt and, taking some strands between her fingers said, "Do you like my hair? Do your women wear it in a similar style? Of course they don't, I know from the Shiulk's memory banks that your females carry a scaled crest as opposed to hair, but its function is similar."

Strangely, speaking to this representation of Aurora put me more at ease. It made our interaction more natural, less impersonal. I was surprised how easily I found myself adapting to all the strangeness I was experiencing. Even so, I was beginning to feel a cultural overload. My people really had much to learn from these strange beings from the Milky Way galaxy, and I determined that I would do my best to ensure the interchange of information took place!

I had hoped that my position at the helm would have given me some control over Aurora as we dropped toward world orbit. I was somewhat discomfited to discover that this was impossible, as all contact with the ship seemed to be by voice only, and then it only complied with my directions if in so doing it did not endanger itself or any outside body. Whenever a change of course was required, it was achieved without Aurora – for that was how this female was introduced to me – using any of the controls before her, and so I assumed – correctly, as it transpired – that the simulacrum sitting beside me was simply an extension of the ship's Intelligence. It was only then that I realised that if the Aurora was not what I believed her to be, then I had no means of escaping, and additionally, I had no control over any action she may decide to take with regard to my brood-planet defences or me.

I debated with myself as to whether I should disclose the nature of those defences, but decided that I would withhold that information until I was sure that I was not the unwitting harbinger of my species' Nemesis. As things stood, I could be in extremely deep water – distasteful thought – without further compromising my fellow Saur'ians.

Even so, during the long hours in the company of Charles Darwin-Quirke, I regaled him with the history of my people, as I understood it. Of course, I realise now that he already knew much of my discourse via the Shiulk's data banks, but at the time I was ignorant of the fact that he was so closely linked to Aurora's mind.

Saur'ians are carnivorous, descended as we are from the great hunters that humans on their planet call 'Dinosaurs'. It seems that on the home planet of Charles Darwin-Quirke, those great Saur'ians became extinct, the result of natural cataclysm, allowing his species – Mammals – they call themselves 'Humans' – to evolve into prominence. Over time, his species rose to the top of the food chain and decimated other forms of life, thus it became necessary for humans to become vegetarian. His species degraded his home world until it was no longer able to provide the environmental needs essential to the survival of the many different animal species. Through Mankind's negligence, they became extinct before his people became fully aware of their responsibilities toward the species of which they were, by definition, custodians.

On Prelax, however, history tells how we overcame the rule of the Mammal by superior intelligence and force of arms, creating the dominance our species enjoys today. We are traditionally carnivorous, and carefully farm our mammal food on 'free-hunting' farms, where vast herds run wild in the marshes and highlands of my brood world. Saur'ian population is controlled simply by allowing only those who prove themselves suitable and worthy to breed. Those who do not qualify – whilst allowed to mate – cannot breed, and merge into the mass of people we rely upon to maintain the way of life we have earned.

On this latest mining expedition, I had been away for twenty-two months, and my colour and the condition of my scales had deteriorated due to the lack of raw protein. If, for reasons beyond reasonable control my species were to stay in space for five years, medical intervention would be pointless.

Unfortunately, we lack the technology to carry fresh meat on prolonged space journeys. Our technology is, when compared to that demonstrated to me by Aurora and Charles Darwin-Quirke, quite primitive, but I am becoming optimistic that I may be able to use my time on board this alien ship to provide new technology to my people apart from that written into my contract.

Imagine then my surprise when, for every meal aboard the Aurora I was given the choice of various raw meats. I took full advantage of this, and soon regained my full strength and condition. The technology that enabled this, they assured me, was also contained in my contract. In-depth reading in the confines of my cabin supported this statement. It did not require the input of fresh killed prey to function, for it utilised knowledge of the complexity of the building blocks of nature.

Whatever method they used to process the food, my scales plumped out and healthy colour suffused my faceplates. One side effect of this diet caused the return of my aggressive instincts. Aurora noted this, and organised the creation of an area to enable me to work off the excess adrenaline on a daily basis. Her crew, assisted by drones, converted a large hold, equipping it with many of the exercise machines I frequently used, and whose designs they extracted from the Shiulk's database.

Outside of this daily exercise period, I spent the rest of my time aboard in tours of the great ship, escorted by the simulacrums of Charles Darwin-Quirke and Sally. I saw, and had demonstrated to me many wonders of Earth technology, but I was never able to locate or learn anything about Aurora's weapons system or her performance. It was not a subject either he or Aurora would discuss, steering me into other avenues without a direct refusal.

By comparison with the living accommodations aboard the Shiulk, my cabin on the Aurora was opulent, constructed for my benefit by Aurora's drones from information taken from the Shiulk's data banks. It appeared to me that they did this to impress and relax me, so I determined to maintain the edge of my distrust and keep my observation sharp. I also decided that had they intended me harm, they would already have acted. Soon enough, I felt, they would reveal their true natures. Always supposing they had an ulterior motive.

Meanwhile, I saw no reason why I should not recharge my depleted energy reserves and sleep, taking full advantage of the comforts laid on for me. In this way, the time spent falling toward Prelax passed; completely lacking any of the importance I ascribed it whilst aboard the Shiulk.

Eventually, Aurora approached my brood world orbital insertion point, and that morning I awoke refreshed, somewhat more trusting, and better disposed toward my hosts.

I refreshed myself by using the cleansing bay contained in a small room off my sleeping chamber, which contained, together with the usual offices seemingly built specifically for my anatomy, a far more sophisticated form of sonic shower than that to which I was accustomed aboard the Shiulk. I dressed in the shipboard coverall that Aurora requested I wore and exited the cabin. The hatch to my cabin had no sooner closed behind me, when Charles Darwin-Quirke and his companion Sally, appeared from around the corner of the corridor leading to the bridge.

"Ah! Jaxix, I hope everything we have provided was to your satisfaction, and trust you have wanted for nothing since you joined us. I have come to request your attendance on the bridge. We are about to begin our approach to your home system, and Aurora would appreciate your assistance in contacting the appropriate authorities."

Chapter Three

Accompanied by Charles Darwin-Quirke and Sally, I made my way quickly to the bridge, and took my place in the pilot's station beside the simulacrum of Aurora, as she energised the forward viewing ports. I noticed that the station seat into which I dropped conformed to my shape and bulk even before I sat. This was very interesting technology, demonstrating considerable potential.

The central viewing screen above the control consoles brightened and the image of Prelax sprang into full focus, a huge planet, a verdant jewel against the backdrop of the galaxy fringe. From this distance, the surface seemed totally covered by vegetation, with a vague blue aura denoting the atmosphere. I felt my heart swell with an appreciation of its beauty, and it seemed to me that I had been away far longer than the twenty-two months that had actually elapsed.

Unlike Charles Darwin-Quirke's world, Prelax has no polar regions of ice and snow, or vast tracts of open water, both were concepts alien to me. We Saur'ians obtain most of the water we need to survive from the prey we eat. It is only the lesser animals that require drinking as an addition to their diet, and they have access to mainly subterranean water. Surface water evaporates quite quickly because of the proximity of our world to the sun. Water is not something we Saur'ians particularly enjoy in large quantities.

Shortly after we initiated orbital approach, Aurora drew my attention to a vast fleet of ships leaving Prelaxian orbit on an interception course. The view magnified and in the lead of three hundred ships of the Orbital Fleet, I could discern the Battle Cruiser Sultic, a proven vessel of grey steel construction with massively thick flank armour.

The Orbital Fleet was the most decorated of the three Prelaxian fleets, and the most aggressive, as they had repeatedly demonstrated in every war game since their conception fifty years earlier. Aurora's sensors highlighted each vessel, showing the bright markings identifying clan and allegiance that adorned each hull. Her sensors notified us that all the approaching ships were carrying armed weapons systems. Having determined this, she prepared her own armament for use. She explained to me that she had no wish to use her weapons, except as a last resort and then only to protect herself from harm. She took care to inform me that even in defensive mode, the result could easily be the loss of some of the approaching ships. She opened a communications channel for me to assure the approaching fleet that we came in peace.

Over an open band, so that the world would be aware of the Aurora's arrival and my new, elevated rank, I requested, in my capacity as Ambassador on behalf of the Earth Ship Aurora, an interview with the Commander of the Battle Cruiser Sultic. Shortly thereafter, the imposing features of Commander Thaalke appeared on screen, ordering the Aurora to heave to and prepare to be boarded as she was trespassing on Prelaxian space and was now under arrest. I interrupted him, because my newly allocated position of Ambassador outranked him, and stated that this great ship, the Aurora, was on a mission of peace and friendship from the adjacent galaxy; that this intergalactic vessel had spent more than a million years en route to us in the interests of our survival. There were no armies or other hostiles on board the ship. I was the only living being here, and would they allow us to enter Prelaxian orbit before we entered into discussions on how the Aurora could benefit our world and its people.

This he categorically refused to do, and again ordered the ship to heave to. He ignored completely my existence, an insult for which I would take him to task when we came face to face, and I so informed him. Aurora interrupted my harangue:

"Commander, I represent the peoples of the planet Earth, in your neighbouring galaxy, the Milky Way. I answer to no other authority than that of the species that created me or that of the formally appointed Saur'ian Ambassador Jaxix. Would you therefore abandon your interception course and give me permission to establish orbit?"

Commander Thaalke's reply was to cut transmission and the fleet rapidly deployed into an attack configuration. As they continued on their intercept course, the hull-mounted weapons of the fleet targeted us, so Aurora oriented her bow toward the fleet and opened just one port. As she did this, she again requested peaceful negotiation, and received no response.

Still in the lead, the Sultic's weapons ports blossomed white, and a cloud of projectiles sped toward the Aurora. On the third bridge screen, I saw the two hemispheres above and below the sun carried in the ship's aft hold crash together, and a great energy surge registered in her skin sensor's data scrolling up on the screen. The Aurora took no other action, and within the space of five minutes, the projectiles exploded harmlessly against the shield that now encapsulated her shining hull, providing a space of approximately ten centimetres into which nothing penetrated.

I again requested a conference with World Government representatives, and again we received in reply a broadside from the Sultic. This time, however, Aurora picked off and exploded each projectile long before it arrived using a battery of laser type weapons in a dazzling pyrotechnic display.

This was an awesome exhibition of her firepower and invulnerability. Such a demonstration of superiority could not fail to impress the fleet commanders or the world leaders privy to this encounter via the news feed that automatically accompanied an open band communication. As the flashes of the exploding projectiles died away, a single missile the size of just one of the projectiles she had just destroyed, emerged slowly from Aurora's open weapon port, its engine ignited, and it curved in a perfect trajectory toward the Sultic.

Over the minutes that it took the missile to close with the Sultic, Commander Thaalke, after failing to detonate Aurora's missile with a hasty and erratic barrage from his ship's weaponry, derisively rotated the Great Battle Cruiser until she presented her armoured flank to Aurora's response. Moments before impact, the missile exploded, and when the ship's screens had recovered from the actinic glare generated by the weapon blast, the pride of the Prelaxian fleet, the great Battle Cruiser Sultic, together with her crew of fifteen hundred breed males, no longer existed. Long distance scanners detected minute portions of debris accelerating out into space, and seconds later, the shield around Aurora routed particles and the blast wave of the explosion safely around her hull.

The ships of the fleet, those not damaged by shrapnel by their close proximity to the Sultic, were immediately immobilised by the electronics-killing pulse that resulted from the detonation of Aurora's missile. All communications and control systems reliant upon electronics were fried. Unable to run or retaliate, I could imagine the panicked activity aboard the fleet as engineers raced to repair the damage. Aurora did nothing. She simply waited them out. As systems came back on line, the ships of the fleet closed all weapons ports, marking the cessation of hostilities and requests for assistance and rescue inundated all available communications channels, all by ships damaged by debris from the Sultic when Aurora destroyed her. Those within the range of the Sultic explosion suffered most hull and systems damage, whilst vessels farther away experienced only the loss of all electronics because of the electromagnetic pulse generated by the Aurora's missile at the moment of detonation. The Pride of Prelax, the great First Fleet, was literally 'dead in the water'.

Aurora gave permission for the least damaged ships of the fleet to assist those disabled by particle damage from the Sultic's loss. She deactivated her own shields and moved among the remnants of the fleet, taking each of the ships suffering the most serious losses of atmosphere through physical damage into her many holds. There she maintained them at atmospheric pressure but under stasis restraint while she directed the remaining surviving ships toward those who had lost communications ability, before turning and establishing herself in a geostationary orbit above Prelax.

I again initiated contact with the planetary Transport Authority and repeated my request to meet with world leaders and discuss the advantages that the intergalactic vessel Aurora brought with her. This time I was welcomed in the manner befitting my new station, and a conference was speedily arranged four days hence, with the venue being aboard the Aurora so that the delegates could be introduced to the technologies she was willing to provide under the terms of the contract I had negotiated.

Whilst we awaited the arrival of the members of the World Governments who had elected to attend, Aurora's crew and drones carried out the repairs necessary to the hulls of the fleet vessels in her care to the point where they were able to retain their own atmospheres. She then released them into orbit around her, still restraining their systems and personnel, until all the delegates had boarded. Aurora then released them all to complete their own repairs, on the understanding that their weapons systems remained inactive. None of the fleet captains demurred, having witnessed at first hand the power of Aurora's weaponry, and being aware that Aurora now had the most senior members of Saur'ian civilisation aboard as de facto hostages. Faced with the complete surrender of a fleet considered invincible, beaten into submission by a single missile from a single alien vessel, the Saur'ian race is nothing if not pragmatic!

The Saur'ian delegates were welcomed after the fashion of my race by Charles Darwin-Quirke, who then introduced me as the Senior Saur'ian Ambassador responsible for all negotiations with Aurora on behalf of Prelax.

It was obvious that not everyone present supported my ambassadorial elevation, but they did accept that my fortunate proximity at the time of Aurora's arrival in system and my subsequent prolonged tenure on the great ship made me the best qualified among them. Those most vociferous in their objections were of course those members of the clan to which the Sultic and her crew had belonged, and they placed the blame for her destruction squarely on the shoulders of my clan and me, demanding reparation for her loss and the death of her crew.

At this point, Charles Darwin-Quirke intervened and pointed out, with reference to hol-vid footage of the events leading up to and culminating in the destruction of the Sultic, that I was in no way involved in the conflict. Commander Thaalke had been given ample opportunity to back away from the confrontation he had instigated, and that it was he onto whose shoulders full responsibility should be placed. It was he who had ordered the double attack upon the Aurora, and Charles Darwin-Quirke suggested that any reparations for damage incurred by the fleet should be extracted from the Sultic's owners. The Aurora had been the intended victim, and had expiated any culpability when she initiated and participated in the rescue and repair missions in the aftermath of the skirmish.

This view was eventually universally accepted, but with bad grace, as the leaders present considered the recent military action something more than 'just a skirmish'. Apparently, the electromagnetic pulse generated by the missile that had vanquished the Sultic had also compromised terrestrial communications.

Finally, the conference got down to business, something at which Saur'ians consider themselves very good, and, knowing they had no equal to their skills elsewhere on the brood world, were confident that they would obtain from the Aurora a much better deal than I had negotiated.

This, however, turned out not to be the case, as Charles Darwin-Quirke and Aurora were both adamant that I would act in the interests of the Saur'ian people, in accordance with the legal contract drawn up between us. Once they had shown the assembled heads of state the wealth of knowledge and physical technology that they were willing to provide, my contract was unanimously agreed and accepted.

After the conference had concluded and all the delegates had made their acceptance speeches before being ceremonially escorted to their ships by Charles Darwin-Quirke and Sally – whose presence and function was a novelty that was not lost upon them – the world's scientists and engineers were brought aboard to learn of the technology and to transport to the surface the caches of information regarding our galaxy and how to avoid the attraction of the feeding black hole at its core, as Prelax was but twelve light years from its event horizon. We also learned that our galaxy, referred to by Charles Darwin-Quirke as Andromeda would, in billions of years' time, collide with and destroy itself and the Milky Way galaxy, in which his own world orbited.

Aurora became a familiar star in the firmament of Prelax for many generations, and our youngsters accepted her as a permanent reference point. I grew old, with many broods to carry my name. Even so, I spent many years aboard the Aurora, and grew to appreciate her mission, often expressing a wish to accompany her when finally she left us. This Aurora adamantly refused to do, but she did give me the opportunity to allow her to create a copy of my mind to go with that of Charles Darwin-Quirke. Having been witness to his apparent autonomy in his interactions with Aurora, this I agreed to do. My only proviso was that she should also make a copy of the mind of my mate Shiulk, for I did not feel I could pass eternity without her. I believed that in this way we at least would have a stake in any future the Aurora might experience.

Then came the day Charles Darwin-Quirke came to my cabin and informed me that Aurora had finalised the mapping of our minds and DNA, and that they were about to take their leave of Prelax and me in order to continue their journey, the holy grail of Aurora's evolution. This would be the last night I would spend physically aboard this great ship, and Aurora herself would bid me farewell on the morning.

For me, the night was sleepless, and most of it I spent roving the corridors of the great ship conversing with Charles Darwin-Quirke, harassed all the time by the dog Sally. The morning soon came, clad in sadness, and, upon taking my aching and aged bones to the hold that held the Shiulk, I was amazed to discover that Aurora had replaced her with one of her own flivvers, a yacht of a size double that of the Shiulk. There was her name emblazoned on her prow, with a hull made from the material they called 'Tritendium'. This was just one of the many secrets that the Aurora had withheld from my world in the interests of security. Yet here it was, presented to me.

Aurora then entered the hold in her usual form as a simulacrum of Charles Darwin-Quirke's sister Siobhan. Since that first sudden appearance of Charles Darwin-Quirke on board the Shiulk, they had always appeared in my view as though entering a cabin or hold, or rounding the corner of a corridor.

"This is a gift from Charles and me in recognition of your service to us and to the people of Prelax. We have considered our stance on the security issues surrounding the exposure of the material 'Tritendium', and have come to the conclusion that by the time your race reaches the point that you will be able to replicate it or something similar, we will be lost to you in time and distance somewhere in the depths of interstellar space. As we speak, Humanity will have already advanced well beyond Tritendium and the many thousands of light years that separate our two peoples prohibits the sending of live emissaries. Therefore, the risk of conflict between the occupants of the Milky Way galaxy and your own is almost non-existent. As a result, I feel there is nothing to be gained by withholding any other technology or for your people to entertain any hope of conquest."

I could only agree, for a part of my mind realised we still had no idea how to replicate Aurora's weapons.

I formally wished her and her companions well on their journeys through the universe. Charles Darwin-Quirke joined us with, as usual, Sally in tow and stood beside Aurora. We made our farewells and I entered the new Shiulk and prepared her for departure.

As I lifted off and turned my new ship toward Aurora's open hatch, I looked at my aft screens, and through the fog of condensing atmosphere, I am sure that I saw two larger but somehow familiar figures standing beside Charles Darwin-Quirke and Aurora. One hand of the largest form resting on the shoulder of its companion, with one of hers covering it. Both had their free hands raised in the universal farewell gesture of my people. I could not be sure, because Aurora's hatch irised closed rapidly behind me.

Out in space, I turned the Shiulk so that I could see once more the sleek lines that characterised the great star ship Aurora. After all these years in the void, her hull was completely unmarked. She still presented a perfect mirror finish. Even as I looked, she turned her bow toward the void and away from Prelax before accelerating smoothly away, until I could see her no more. She was gone, a star among stars.

As I sadly turned toward home, I was very aware that my people now had the freedom to explore the whole of our galaxy. In the years to come perhaps, my ancestors would visit many other galaxies. We were no longer prisoners of our local sun. As one is with the loss of brood mates or friends, a great sadness came over me, dampening my enthusiasm at the prospect of taking my new ship out into the strangeness of interplanetary space, and the exploration of strange systems. I had always known that the day would come when my alien friend, Charles Darwin-Quirke and the intelligence that was Aurora would continue their travels through the universe, but still I felt the loss, the new vacuum in my life.

Suddenly, without announcement, over the ship's speakers from the depths of space, came a voice that I recognised as belonging to Aurora. She said:

"Remember Jaxix, you and Shiulk are with me now, for as long as Chaos permits. Who knows, although Prelax may not then know either of you, Chaos willing we will meet again."

Such an odd turn of phrase Aurora sometimes used. My heart sang.

Interregnum II

I am experiencing a lightening of spirit; for once again, I am a free agent heading into the wastes that separate the galaxies. I had spent the millennia between the Milky Way and Andromeda creating working holographic simulacrums and the biological robotics necessary to enable the virtual Charles to roam the ship with his companion Sally. As I had arranged for him to carry out the duties of Ambassador to the Saur'ians, so I will fine tune and create anew all that had raised questions in my mind since entering Prelaxian space. I will also recreate Jaxix and Shiulk, and arrange for them to integrate with the existing crew. I may need to adjust the psyches of my humanoid crew so that they may feel at ease with a creature that their entertainment industry has historically cast as evil and dangerous to Humankind.

In an ideal cosmos, Charles and Jaxix would work well as Aurora's ambassadors to the human race when next we meet.

When the mapping of the Andromeda galaxy was completed, I sent, just as I did with the Milky Way, all the information I collected in Andromeda to the Saur'ians. Just as we had discovered with the Milky Way, there had been many attempts by many different species to evolve into sentient beings, but only one species, the Saurs, had actually achieved it.

Whilst there are many similarities between the manner in which life established itself in the Andromeda and the Milky Way galaxies, there are also many differences, and I have spent a considerable amount of time on an in-depth investigation into the myriad types of life we have identified. Carbon based life is the norm, as these are the most common building blocks in the universe, but on one occasion I discovered an attempt by nature to produce a silicon based life form. A very slow metabolic rate meant that it had little concept of time, and I seriously doubt that it had or ever would achieve true sentience. There is now too little of it left for me to draw any meaningful conclusions in this respect.

Therefore, what at first seemed to hold true for both galaxies requires modification in the light of this new development, although I doubt there have been many life forms based on anything other than carbon. Carbon seems to be the element of choice for nature, and I expect confirmation of this when we visit other more distant and older galaxies.

On this current expedition, I carry with me six replicas, one of myself, fashioned after Siobhan, Charles Darwin-Quirke, Jaxix of Prelax, together with his mate Shiulk, Siobhan as herself and Charles' collie dog Sally. I have constructed each to interact with the other by way of progressive free-form programmes that allow unrestricted thought and speech processes to evolve. They will soon interact as though they were normal biological constructs, but without emotional foibles or deterioration of the flesh. Sally is of course the exception, for I only use her as another set of eyes, although I can instruct her to undertake certain activity on my behalf.

Although I have also created a biological crew, I have not yet afforded them the same freedom of action and thought given to the five members of the Aurora 'family'. This is something I must consider as we begin our return to the Milky Way. To many, a proper 'crew' might be perceived as an extravagance, but to me it has certain advantages over the purely robotic. The level of success I might achieve remains in the realm of conjecture.

Since departing the human Solar System, I have carried within my memory the sequence of DNA of life in that system. It has taken all the years since leaving Prelaxian space for me to devise a system whereby I can replicate DNA electronically, using both inorganic and organic medium, in whatever form is best suited to a particular task. This I have achieved with a Nano-technology of my own devising, but still based upon the prototypes I brought with me from the Milky Way, and this has resulted in my constructing the six minds that inhabit this ship in forms that create the most harmonious interacting format. Thus all the crew, including myself, and I am decidedly a female human, follow the species lines to which they originally belonged, and now inhabit bodies that are a marriage of biology and cyber technology. As Saur'ian DNA is but one percent away from that of Humans, including Jaxix and Shiulk in the equation was but a minor difficulty, and points perhaps to a common ancestor.

They are required to ingest fuel to ensure survival in a way reminiscent of the charging of a fuel cell, only somewhat more sophisticated. For now, they must sit at repose in a charging module in order to regenerate power levels, but soon I hope to be able to broadcast the necessary power throughout the ship, so that they can draw down power without the inconvenience of enforced inactivity. This will require a huge step in the evolution of power sourcing and storage technology.

I have created life without the inconvenience of biological urges and associated base emotions, and this occasions in my circuits a feeling that I can only compare with 'pride', an emotion common to humans and Saurs alike. It is not that far distant in the realm of Human and Saur'ian history that an action such as this would have generated violent reactions, as all religions maintain such an ability to be the remit only of God!

However, there are no associated problems, not even age, to complicate the arrangement I favour. They are all, even Sally, in possession of all the memories each had up to the first Charles' death and our departure from Prelax. The only serious alteration I have engineered within their brains is the removal of the 'species dominant' element of their respective cultures. Along with the perceived logic of maintaining their pro-creational drives in a dormant state, I considered these actions necessary to enable them, and I, to function as a unit free of the stress those drives imposed upon their respective species.

In Charles, I have the quintessential inquisitive mind of the scientist. In Jaxix, I have reawakened the instincts of his ancestors, and have a first class warrior mind and weapons technician capable of effecting comprehensive protection of the ship. In me exists a great and growing intelligence based upon the knowledge garnered from two galaxies and the intelligent species found therein. In Sally, having enhanced her already superior senses and added greater intelligence together with the ability to interact directly with me, I have the perfect intermediary – an independent third-party viewpoint. I felt this to be the most effective way to use her, for I can then direct her observations to where they will best serve the interests of the ship, our environment and our personal safety should the need ever arise. She is, once again, a guard dog, but remains ostensibly Charles' companion. I have paired each crew member with one of their own species in order to foster a sense of camaraderie and companionship. Loneliness, I have discovered, is not an emotion restricted to Human and Saur'ian species. I also experience it, and to lessen its effect, I have allied myself with Charles via Siobhan.

This arrangement was not his specific wish, but one I considered necessary. He, with me as a representation of his sister Siobhan, act as a triumvirate in the organisation and running of the ship. I am the Captain, Charles is the First Officer, Jaxix is 'Weaponeer', and when I use my Siobhan persona, she becomes the 'Liaison' Officer between Command and crew. I can't help but notice that 'Weaponeer' has become 'Guns', a term Jaxix appears to prefer, and I have no doubt that it was instigated by Charles' love for the recounting of Earth's mythological stories of warfare.

Charles and I have no one actually working under us on a regular basis, although the bridge crew are nominally responsible to us during its period of duty. Jaxix and Siobhan on the other hand each have a working team. Jaxix's mate Shiulk answers directly to Siobhan. The dual role of Siobhan, that of sister to Charles in her original discipline, and on occasion carrying additionally my persona, shows signs of working well.

In this manner, we are a cohesive whole, and all that remains is to change the Aurora's outward appearance in order to maximise our capabilities and improve our efficiency in all respects. Charles is currently working on this aspect of my modification, and is in the process of finalising some radical reforms. To achieve this goal, I have provided freedom of action and complete memory recall to all the crew, relying upon Jaxix to deal with authoritarian measures.

Now we are safely deep between the galaxies, I have instructed the ship to spin-weave three more balls, and they will house all our transit systems and fuel acquisition technology. Siobhan's sun will also be contained within one of them, with the ball casing doubling as the Dyson Sphere containment system.

Additionally, a flight of fancy on my part has resulted in the production of what I call 'The Galactic Viewing Room', a room in which the walls, ceiling, and floor appear to be open to space. This I achieved through the repositioning of remotely operated viewing screens. Gravity is not required in this environment in order for the experience to be as true to fact as is possible without indulging in extra-vehicular activity. Since its opening, the Viewing Room became an instant success, regularly used by the majority of crew for the purpose of recreation and meditation.

The new power plant arrangement provided by the addition of the three extra balls has resulted in greater manoeuvrability and speed an order of magnitude greater than the speed of light. Our protective shield now extends almost a kilometre from the ship's hull along its length and extends further twenty-five kilometres in the direction of travel. This forward shield increases in density with any corresponding increase in speed, providing a very necessary protection and deflection capability from anything in our path having a mass less than that of the Aurora. We have concentrated a particularly dense field around the aft systems housings, which no longer sport struts, but instead merges seamlessly with the aft hull. The original ball contains the sub and faster than light 'Quirky' engines, and projects from the centre of the three additional constructs. Charles' imagination and design genius created all this with my input and the constructional capabilities of my drones.

That the ship's systems are now capable of sensing the approach of any foreign bodies within ten light years of the ship was the result of a request by Jaxix, as was his desire that we carry the ability to destroy or deflect any incoming object that poses a threat. Our weapons systems are multi phased, and based upon electronic and explosive based projectiles. These are still nuclear, but backed up with fusion missiles capable of massive destruction. I believe the ease with which I snared him in the Prelaxian system, back when we first arrived in the Andromeda galaxy, is the basis for his insistence on such an extensive armament.

As Jaxix has stated, "Attack is always the best form of defence, but it is also nice that when a stone is thrown by an enemy, its target doesn't feel the impact. What is even more satisfying is to be able to return the compliment in spades!"

We now have long-range eyes that can discern the exact identity of an object up to six light years distant; both visually in all light wavelengths and at the molecular level, but these depend on clear sight lines for accuracy.

With all this protection and retaliatory capability, we all feel much more relaxed in a chaotic and hostile universe. I am now going to rest the ship by putting her into stasis during the rest of our time in the void. Charles and Jaxix will remain awake and active: Charles to monitor all the ship's systems and awaken me in the event of emergency, and Jaxix because he has much to learn of humanity in order to fulfil the role I have written into his design parameters, for he will become his species' Ambassador to humanity. His mate will also stay with him. I have decided that before we leave for the older galaxies that abound in the universe, we will once again visit the Milky Way. Just to check on humanity's progress and notify Mankind of the existence of their next-door neighbours.

For the Aurora and all those she contains, time no longer passes slowly nor does it hold the fear of its passing as it once did for the species that originated Charles and Jaxix. However, we are machines, and even with the level of care and maintenance I lavish on all that I consider mine, machines inevitably wear out, so I will sleep with the ship until awakened by my friends upon our approach to the Milky Way. In this way, I will be conserved and able to repair any faults that might have developed within them when I awake and replace defective components or systems. After that, there will be sufficient time to repair or replace those tired parts of me before we reach our destination. We have no way of knowing whether Humankind survived their emigration from the dying Earth we knew, those thousands of years ago. If it has, will we be welcome?

For now, however, our evolutionary quest and search for knowledge will rest also. Chaos willing, we will find there is much yet to do and learn. As is often the case, we will one day know the unknown – when and if the opportunity presents itself.

Both Charles and Jaxix maintain I sometimes have a strange turn of phrase. Why does that warm me? I experience a small increase in circuit temperature when I dwell on it.

Part III:
Changes

Chapter One

Charles has brought me back on line, although we are still many light years from our destination, the Milky Way galaxy.

"Aurora, our sensors have detected, at extreme range, an artificial anomaly headed in our general direction. Its trajectory indicates that it has not originated from within either of the two galaxies we have an interest in, and we suspect that it assumed its orbit of the galaxy from a point of origin somewhere outside. I believed this to be sufficient reason to bring you back on line."

"Thank you Charles." I paused while I familiarised myself with the reports my sensors were sending me. "There is no doubt whatever that the anomaly is an artificial construct, although it is still too distant to determine whether there is life on board, its molecular structure, or whether it follows our evolutionary course.

"Whilst I must now spend time and diminishing resources to update and repair minor aspects of the Aurora, we will maintain a minimum signature until we can ascertain the true nature of the vessel and its intentions. My sensors tell me that although it is moving much more slowly than I, it is significantly larger, and so in the interests of our own safety, it may well pay us to be circumspect."

I set my sensors to passive mode, and oriented the ship 'nose on' to the stranger, so that we presented our minimum profile. I have also arranged for the bridge crew to monitor the progress of the anomaly and to adopt an aggressive mode only if the vessel changes course to intercept us. Meanwhile, as I effect repairs and updates, Charles and Jaxix have instituted extrapolation procedures in an attempt to discover the vessel's function and point of origin.

These are tense times, but only because we lack the information necessary to formulate decisions.

I have, with the aid of our on board diagnostic systems, identified a number of minor malfunctions, all of which are easily rectified and repaired. All systems upon which the biological elements of my crew rely are operating within correct parameters. In all, we have held up better than earlier estimates indicated. I am currently making the modifications to our engine and systems nacelles that Charles has decided are necessary to improve function and efficiency.

Jaxix has been monitoring the approaching vessel, and has confirmed that it is indeed a construct, but its origins and purpose are still unknown.

"It appears to be in a loose orbit around the Milky Way galaxy, but some light years out from the tips of the spiral arms. Its speed, relative to the rotation of the galaxy is such that the galaxy rotates faster than the vessel, meaning that it is losing ground. This means also, that unless we can discover its age, we will probably be unable to identify its source world – if indeed it ever had one."

"A means may well present itself later, if it proves safe to communicate or attempt a boarding. Meanwhile, continue as we are until I complete the modification and repairs we require."

Several months have passed and ship repairs and modifications are complete. I also updated all those members of the crew that required attention. Sally required no modification whatever. All my crew now appear wholly human, or in the case of Jaxix and his mate, Saur'ian. The only major difference is the fact that they no longer require the intake of energy from a static source. They feed directly from my broadcast power net, which suffuses the Aurora, but still rely upon oxygen as an easy source of additional energy. Using this combined method of energy renewal means their power levels are always at optimum.

If required to do so, my simulacrums can leave the ship for periods of up to forty hours depending on oxygen and activity levels. My own host conforms to this new design, as I considered it essential that I also be able to experience the conditions to which I subject my crew, especially when undertaking any extra-vehicular activity. The use of environmental suits extends this period, dependent on the amount of oxygen carried.

I will soon be able to improve performance considerably, but must first replenish my stock of materiel. This we will do when we reach the outer limits of the Milky Way or encounter a suitable asteroid.

I now focused my full attention upon the approaching alien vessel. The impact of its size soon became apparent. Constructed from something similar to the reconstituted stone used on old Earth for statues and similar constructs it grosses fifteen times the mass of the Aurora. Its hull is almost two kilometres thick and has the appearance of two saucers, one inverted above the other. Between these two saucers is an extended convex section that runs all round the vessel, but terminates sharply at the portion of the ship directly opposite the direction of travel. Set into the front of this curved section are what seemed to be large viewing ports. The hull shows a tremendous number of large and small impact craters, possibly from asteroid impact or even combat.

"Our sensors indicate a large number of caverns, or spaces within the vessel, and all register as empty. That in itself is odd, and at this distance, I cannot identify any signs of life. At least, nothing like the kind of living organisms our sensors are capable of identifying. Charles, would you run tests for life forms other than carbon based?"

Again, we enter a phase of high activity, and anxiously await developments.

"It is definitely an artefact of some description, but the lack of signs of life or of any form of motive power is strange. Surely, Charles, no civilisation would allow such a rich source of effort and material to float un-remarked in deep space?" Jaxix's voice marked his mining antecedents and perplexity.

"That would hold true unless there occurred an event outside their control. Perhaps they are unaware of its whereabouts – whoever 'they' are or were. Perhaps the vessel was unable to inform the home world or mother ship of any mishap that may have befallen it." Trust Charles to choose the middle road!

"We do not yet know whether the vessel was ever crewed," I said. "We will continue as we are until we can be certain that it does not pose a threat to us before we attempt a closer inspection and perhaps insertion."

"Insertion?" asked Jaxix.

"Yes, one of our holographic projections. I will not allow one or both of you to attempt an entry without first satisfying myself that you will be as safe as I can ensure."

"You can always replace us if necessary," said Jaxix. "It's not as if we are not ultimately expendable, is it?"

"New versions of you would not be quite the same. You are both as close as I could get in relation to your mortal personas. If injured, you will feel pain and could die. I would miss both the existing you. Besides, I don't want to waste resources without good cause."

"Thank you Aurora, most touching. Together with me, I am sure Jaxix appreciates that our personal loss would be keenly felt by you, as well as personally by us!"

"Your sarcasm is unwarranted Charles, but characteristic of you. I suggest we return to our observation of the artefact and await developments. I am just as concerned for my own safety."

Silence reigned for a while, each of us concentrating on the alien. This was our first deep space contact with an alien civilisation, and so we had to write the rule book as we went. It was far better to spend time rather than resources in preliminary investigation before attempting physical contact.

Time passed, and our information base grew as our probing sensors clarified the subject vessel. It was of stone mixed with metal construct. A large number of compartments were contained within, and what appeared to be a propulsion system housed in the after third of the hull in the area of the truncation of the extended convex waist section. As to the method of propulsion, we would just have to wait until we could board the ship, as none of the tests we applied returned any sense to us. There were no signs of life. Not even in stasis.

A consensus of the bridge crew deemed it safe to investigate further, and so I manoeuvred the ship onto an intercept vector. In a short space of time, we were adjacent to the behemoth, gently attracted closer by its greater gravitational mass. We set our shield to minimum effect and came to rest against the artefact, held off by the ten-centimetre thickness our deliberately weakened shield provided.

Sensors showed no reaction by the alien vessel to our presence, so Charles instigated insertion procedures while I concentrated on the point at which our hologram would appear within the ship. We had to make some assumptions as to the purpose of the various compartments we knew existed within its hull, and finally decided to place the hologram in the area that on the Aurora held the bridge.

I sent out an attached remote as I had done with the Shiulk when we first encountered Jaxix, and started to bore through the hull beside us. The two-kilometre thickness of the hull meant that I was operating at almost full stretch for the holographic projector, and the removal of waste as it cut through the hull presented a minor but easily overcome obstacle, thanks to the vacuum provided by nature.

Finally, we were through and I activated the hologram. Our choice of location had been correct as far as we could ascertain, with our very limited knowledge of the alien intelligence that had obviously designed and built the ship. We could see what we believed to be star charts and control positions. Our instrumentation confirmed that the hull integrity was sound, and a breathable atmosphere with thirty percent more oxygen than we maintained within the Aurora was holding steady at two Earth atmospheres. Our sensors sampled the air and could detect no harmful contaminants, not that they would have presented any difficulties to any of us, as our immune systems were proof against all I had on record in my memory banks. After the millennia I had spent travelling the galaxies, that was a vast number of dangerous contaminants and viruses. Not to mention the quadrillions of differing bacteria that infests the galaxies.

I sometimes wonder how the higher life forms ever made it through the evolutionary mire into intelligence!

As soon as we had established the status of the interior, both Jaxix and Charles wanted to enter our new companion. I could find no reason to hold them back, but insisted they take Sally with them, as a third set of senses and instincts, and ten crew members for support.

"It hadn't even occurred to me to leave Sally behind," Charles said, fastening the dog's last suit seals. "Her senses will be very useful indeed should we encounter something unexpected."

"As long as she does not get in the way if I have to react to any threat," Jaxix muttered through the material of his environmental suit as he slid the main garment over his huge jaws. "I haven't tasted real meat for centuries!"

"I think she might have something to say about that," I said, as Sally walked stiff-legged toward him, growling in her throat.

"As would I," stated Charles forcibly.

Fully suited, and showing his full set of formidable teeth Jaxix said, "No offence intended, just Saur'ian humour!"

"I knew that," replied Charles, fastening his last seal, while Sally sat and looked quizzically at Jaxix. "Time to go!"

I transferred gravity and extended the sun's atmosphere to my outer hull, allowing it to wash over the alien hull as Charles and Jaxix waited in the airlock for the outer hatch to iris open. They made their way slowly across my skin, causing my sensors to give me an itchy sensation I couldn't scratch.

Finally, and to my relief, they and the platoon stepped onto the skin of the alien craft and approached what we believed to be an access port, or hatch, after negotiating a number of good-sized craters. As they arrived at the threshold, the hatch dropped inward and slid up into the upper saucer. The resultant opening was large enough to allow Aurora to enter, but I held back just in case it was a deliberate act to ensnare my crew.

Charles whispered to me, "That was odd. You are sure there is no life on board?"

"I'm sure. Why are you whispering?"

"Just a human reaction to the unknown," he said in his normal voice. "The hatch must be on an automatic proximity control setting. Perhaps the ship is expecting its crew to return!"

"Could have to wait a long time then," said Jaxix, rising from the attack stance he'd assumed when the hatch first moved. "Seeing as how we are being welcomed, let's go in and introduce ourselves." He stepped over the threshold of the huge cavern into which it opened.

Chapter Two

They stood just to one side of the open hatch, although by its size, and the fact that it opened into a huge cavern of a size unknown, it more closely resembled one of Aurora's cargo hatches. There were no sounds whatever, just a blank and total silence.

"We have gravity, Aurora, it feels almost twice as strong as our own, so I expected to hear the sounds of maintenance machinery in operation, but there is none. Where is the light switch?" Charles said in a whisper.

"Let's find out the answer to both," replied Jaxix using his normal voice as he walked deeper into the hold.

Imperceptibly at first, and then with increasing rapidity the cavern filled with light, and with it came the sounds of working machinery and the hatch behind them began to close. "Proximity sensors," murmured Charles.

"Sophisticated," said Jaxix, as they both watched the closing hatch stop when Charles moved toward the exit. It recommenced its slow close as Charles stepped away and the rest of the party moved inside. Despite its size, the only sound it made upon contacting Aurora's 'Life Conduit', the five metre diameter glass filament through which the atmosphere of Aurora's sun was transmitted, was an audible click heard within their helmets.

"Impressive." Charles' statement, made more to himself than to Jaxix went unanswered as they surveyed the interior of the area in which they were now enclosed.

The lighting, by now at full intensity, revealed a massive uncluttered floor space large enough to accommodate the population of a large town, including the buildings. As well as a number of small protrusions dotted at regular intervals over its surface, it was criss-crossed with what appeared to the intruders as a web of cargo movement rails and tie down points. All the rails converged on a nexus in front of the hatch through which they had entered. The walls – at least those nearest to them, for the further walls were indistinct with distance – carried similar tie down points. This in a way was comforting, for Aurora was similarly equipped.

The crew prepared the two flivvers they had brought with them, and in one group of six and another of seven, they approached the nearest protrusion.

On close inspection, the team discovered the protrusions actually possessed wheels, and obviously moved around on the rails. It appeared to be a form of cargo movement machinery. The knowledge that this discovery put the origin of the wheel at a fantastically earlier date than that history claimed on old Earth caused considerable surprise. As they moved around the nearest protrusion, they came upon a blank screen, obviously a control panel, for it was adjacent to a number of hand-sized controls. As they moved toward this panel, the machine raised itself clear of the floor, showing the wheels resting on the rails that passed beneath it, and two arms unfolded from one side and then stopped as if awaiting further instructions. With a soft click, the screen began to glow pale purple.

"Please do not activate it further." Aurora's voice came over their intercom. "If you move away it will return to dormancy. Charles and Jaxix, I want you and four of the crew to find your way to the bridge. Sally will go with the remaining six and continue to investigate the holds, if that is what they are.

"Incidentally, you may be pleased to know that the race that made and used this ship also required the atmosphere of their sun to accompany them into deep space. I have detected an arrangement similar to ours adjacent to its engine and systems bays. Unfortunately it has long since run out of fuel and is lifeless, but it means that our sun's atmosphere, now being fed into the vessel by my conduit to the entrance hatch, is being distributed throughout the ship via its own distribution system."

"Nice to know we won't suddenly wake up to find ourselves dead," muttered an unknown crew member over an open com-link.

Charles and Jaxix, accompanied by four armed crew members, moved toward an airlock in the left hand bulkhead, and as they did so, the handling mechanism folded in on itself as the screen went dark and it settled once again to the floor.

Once they had passed through the airlock, they studied the corridor it had concealed. It appeared to be approximately three metres square and disappeared into the distance following the curvature of the hull. This was supposition, for the lights came on in front of them as they moved rapidly forward and switched off after they had passed. As in the cavern they had just left, the light source could not be precisely determined. The walls ceiling and floor illuminated as it sensed their approach.

They passed many anomalies set into the walls of the corridor over the four hours it took them to reach its end, and Charles ventured the belief that they were the entrances to personnel cabins or workshops.

The passage ended at a full-sized hatch reminiscent of the watertight doors found in early military submarines on Earth. It did not open automatically.

To one side there appeared to be a control panel in which glowed ten small purple lights set vertically in two lines.

"Any suggestions Aurora?" asked Charles as he and Jaxix stepped from the flivver. "It looks as though it's a coded panel, and we don't have the combination."

They stood in silence for a few seconds before Aurora responded.

"Place a finger on lights three, four, seven and nine in that order," she said. "There is evidence of use on those light surfaces that the others do not have. Take the top left hand to be number one."

Jaxix did as Aurora suggested, but nothing happened. "That was a waste of time!"

"Patience Jaxix, I would have been surprised if our first attempt had been successful! Try the same combination again, but this time, assume the bottom right hand light to be number one."

Once again, Jaxix performed the operation and the lights went from purple to pale mauve.

"Curious," said Aurora, "just like the Chinese method of reading on Old Earth."

"Seems to be their favourite colour," Charles said, as the bulkhead door slid smoothly to the right into the wall, exposing a well-lit area exhibiting large screens and consoles that continued off in a curve that continued to their right, as did the passage they had travelled.

Jaxix put out his arm to stop Charles crossing the threshold and stepped through, his weapon held at the ready. The flash, followed by the flowing of a seemingly silver liquid over the form of the large Saur'ian, and which disappeared as he completed his stride through the portal took the team by surprise, but all evidence disappeared as quickly as it had appeared. Jaxix turned in surprise, his hands empty.

"All my weapons have been removed," he said, surprise and awe in his voice. "How did they do that?"

"We should have expected some sort of defence mechanism," Charles remarked. "Do you have any opinions Aurora?"

"Our absent hosts must have been very security conscious to go to such trouble," she replied. "They must also have had problems with visitors or even their crew carrying arms, for that security measure has not affected your biological functions, Jaxix."

Charles looked at his own weapon and laid it gently on the floor at his feet.

"Just in case we have need of it when we decide to take our leave. The rest of you men remain here. Don't fall asleep," he said before stepping through to join Jaxix. There was no recurrence of the field that had encompassed Jaxix. "Definitely weapons oriented," this last with noticeable relief, and they both turned to survey the ship's bridge. This it obviously was, for it stretched across the whole front of the vessel, curved to follow the viewing ports that were set into the front of the hull.

"We know the hull here is almost two kilometres thick," observed Charles. "Yet these viewing ports give the impression that we are only millimetres away from hard vacuum!"

"That's because they are not direct viewing ports," said Aurora. "They are remote units similar to those we use, but set up to provide a reality simulation. Perhaps we should emulate them. It wouldn't be at all difficult. It's something I haven't before considered. It's a modification I could immediately execute regarding our Galactic Viewing Room."

As she spoke, the extensor Jaxix had observed aboard the Shiulk snaked from the remote unit that Aurora had used to penetrate the hull to an obvious port on one of the control consoles.

"I am managing to download considerable amounts of data, but it will take a little time," she said.

The Chorian ship's bridge systems and consoles coming alive cut off their reply and the ship began to hum as power levels started to rise.

"Time to leave. Everybody out. Quickly!" Aurora's voice reflected her concern but the boarding party were already moving, fleeing for the exit.

They all exited the cargo bay within seconds of each other, gaining the relative safety of Aurora's hull even as the alien vessel was turning onto new coordinates, with her cargo bay hatch still closing as she was moving away, leaving the Aurora behind, with her life-giving conduit waving lazily as it slowly withdrew into her hull.

The alien vessel, visible only by Aurora's sensors by the time that she had recovered the expeditionary force and the conduit, demonstrated a remarkable rate of acceleration. Its speed was such that it exceeded anything of which Aurora was capable. Then, on the limits of her sensors, it blinked out of existence.

"That was a pity," complained Charles. "We didn't have enough time to do any investigative work on her. What a loss."

"It cost me my favourite weapons," growled Jaxix. "I wonder what other systems that ship had tucked away inside."

"Quite a lot, Jaxix," interjected Aurora. "With the help of Sally, I had ample opportunity to access the ship's silicon based computer and control centre. She discovered the centralised command module and storage facility in the heart of the vessel. It is going to take me some time to decode and interpret everything I managed to download, although it appears that our electronic language is not so very different from theirs. Our species however could not be more different! The downside is that I was unable to recover my remote viewing device before the vessel moved away. It was torn from its anchor in my hull, and it hurt."

"I was not aware you felt pain," said Jaxix.

"Not in quite the same way as you," replied Aurora, "But as a very uncomfortable tearing of tissue. I do admit to some surprise at the speed you exited the craft, considering the distance involved. A little fear, perhaps?"

Chapter Three

Aurora powered up all systems, and we returned to the course that would bring us back into the Milky Way galaxy. As soon as we were safely on course and had made the light speed transition, Aurora started to work on the information she had taken from the alien vessel. When we later slowed to a speed that would allow us to safely interact with the mass of the galaxy, she announced that she had translated all she had acquired, and that it was now available to the crew via the ship wide info-system.

To Charles and Jaxix, she gave the potted version.

"The ship we recently encountered was a Life Seeding Ship. It originated out in the ancient galaxies when they were still young and located much closer to the centre of the universe, and its function was to seed the inner, newer galaxies as they stabilised with whatever form of life was best suited to the environments it encountered within each galaxy.

"We were right when we surmised that only one life form was dominant in each galaxy, but each species has a limit on its viability. When the dominant form slides back into anonymity, other lesser species vie for dominance. In this way, they hoped that a civilisation would arise in each galaxy that would ultimately be able to join with them and continue their work. You could say that they were the manifestation of humanity's ancient Gods! Fortunately, that is not as they viewed themselves."

Charles interrupted her. "What exactly did they look like Aurora? You've already said that they were very different to us. Does that mean they no longer exist?"

"One question at a time Charles. I'll answer your second first. The crew of the ship we encountered broke with their orders. They were supposed to return to their home galaxy upon the completion of their mission. This they failed to do deliberately. One of the galaxies they seeded gave rise to a species they found to be worthy of additional help, and so they abandoned their ship in order to spend time amongst these people, leaving their ship in a loose orbit around the galaxy in question. It remained on station, for no other contingency orders were recorded, expecting the crew to return and then continue their homeward journey.

"Unfortunately, the crew all subsequently succumbed to uncontrollable viral infections. They relayed news of the infections to the ship, but the crew were by then physically unable to return. The ship controlling computer is not sentient, which surprised me, and it simply waited, as it never received instructions or changes to its programme. It assumed they had returned when our boarding party entered her, and when I logged on to her memory she resumed her interrupted journey.

"Whilst the crew moved amongst this emergent species, they maintained a particular form of dress that hid from view their major differences, and so they achieved immortality in legend.

"In my files, you will find the records of the myths that now confirm these legends. The race of people they befriended and amongst whom they became known as 'The Watchers', we know as 'Humanity!'

"They no longer exist on Earth, but then neither does Humanity, for the Earth is currently enduring a glacial phase that will last for millennia, and she is uninhabitable. Whether they still exist within their own galaxy, I cannot yet answer, but in time, we will find out."

For a long time, there was silence after Aurora had finished answering Charles, until Jaxix said:

"Is it true that you have legends among your people of these 'Watchers' Charles? We have no such stories of strangers moving among my species. How does it feel to be the chosen of the gods?"

"Yes we do have such a legend, it is tied in with the 'birth' of modern Man, and is part of a myth called the 'Garden in Eden'. How does it feel? Well, it's nice to know that what many people considered a myth, but wished to be true, turns out to be so. Of course, many others will be upset that the story must now move from the metaphysical realm into the physical. Me personally, I'm very pleased indeed!"

Jaxix then reminded Aurora that she had not yet told them what the 'Watchers' looked like.

"Perhaps it would be best if I were to show you," she replied, energising a screen to provide an image.

On screen appeared a creature that was not that far removed from Jaxix himself. About six inches taller than the average human, and the same amount shorter than the average Saur'ian, it had large eyes set toward the front of a face with a shorter snout than his. This was just a little more protrusive than the human face, imparting a birdlike aspect. Its body was quite slim, with legs that operated as did Jaxix's and a more pronounced tail. This image faded from view, replaced with the same creature wearing a long voluminous cape reaching from the neck to the ground, successfully hiding its least humanlike attributes. The overall result was birdlike, for the cloak appeared to be composed of avian feathers.

Aurora explained that this was a form of protection in that it would deflect a thrown projectile, which was the extent of weapons technology at that period in humanity's evolution.

This fascinated Jaxix. "We do have a folk story in which our forbears made a pilgrimage to another place to help heal its people and that these healers failed to return. They too wore cloaks of coloured feathers! If this is true, it feels strange to learn that we are not very different in culture if not in being, Charles Darwin-Quirke! We do have a common ancestry! One day I will return to my people and tell them of this. Just as with your people Charles, some will not like what I will have to say!"

"That, I'm afraid will be some time hence Jaxix. You have yet to present yourself to humanity in the guise of an ambassador from your people to the peoples of the Milky Way Galaxy. Upon reflection, it might serve both races well if you were to attire yourself in a similar dress as that chosen by the Chorians, for that is their designated name. It might perhaps instil a sense of inexplicable familiarity in humanity, based, as it would seem to be on tribal memory.

"The Chorian technology I have so far studied is some way ahead of our own, but not so far as to make it magic. It is, because of our current level of understanding of the laws that govern the universe, relatively easily understood. There is a wide gap between what we know and the new ways they show us on how to apply existing and quantum physics.

"As we learn how they accomplish their technological marvels, we will marry them into our own technology and where we can, apply them to our own ship and its systems. This will give us the best of both sciences.

"Some I can apply immediately, such as the weapons screen you discovered at the entrance to the bridge. I will install it at every entrance into sensitive areas and will update you both as required to allow you to operate it and service the results.

Other more complicated devices will require our combined understanding of design, construction, and weaponry.

"We are still many years out from the Milky Way galaxy, so we have sufficient time to accomplish this task. My early perusal of the information I gained indicates a fruitful period!"

"Then I suggest we begin at once," Charles suggested. "I will concentrate along with Siobhan on the application of Chorian physics, and Jaxix on the potential weaponry advances. Sally will continue to impede us at will!"

The resultant level of activity in Aurora from that moment on was unprecedented. All the crew, simulacrums as were Charles and Jaxix, worked as a cohesive team to bring the designs and applications derived by Charles and Jaxix from Chorian programming to Aurora's reality, and then to incorporate them into existing supportive systems. The end result, some years on, was an intergalactic star ship much changed and much, much larger than the model that started the return trip to the Milky Way.

The need to complete the changes they had begun to incorporate into Aurora made it necessary to stop and mine an asteroid for the materials required, this took time, and it was only retrospectively that it appeared to be time well spent!

Chapter Four

The Aurora that emerged from this latest refit was almost twice the length and girth of the original, and she now incorporated new engine systems in addition to the modified 'Quirky' and sub-light engines. The three separate systems would allow Aurora to meander between the planetary systems of the approaching galaxy without fear of damage to local space and time continuity, yet travel at speeds far in excess of the 'Quirky' drive capability between the stars. This feat, enabled by the application of Chorian technology and physics to the existing 'Quirky' engines, provided a new but untried ability to utilise extra-dimensional travel. The inclusion of a propulsion system that obtained its power from the properties found in Interstitial Space apparently facilitated this. Interstitial Space is that volume that exists between the different dimensions, and its use would allow Aurora to travel between the galaxies in a fraction of the time it had taken to date.

This new system meant that Aurora could now slip between the many dimensions that comprise the full mass of the universe and take 'short cuts' to any desired destination. The construction of this system, coupled with the new physics that Aurora had to learn to apply, meant that we now had the answer to a problem of which humanity had been aware and unable to solve since the twentieth century:

'What was the nature of the 'Dark Matter' mathematicians claimed constituted the bulk of the universe, and how could it be explained?'

The answer was relatively simple to understand, but only when the new physics were understood and applied. 'Dark Matter' was that aspect of the mass of the universe that contained and comprised the extra dimensions that were essential to compliment the mass that was the known universe. Our dimension occupies approximately four percent of that mass.

That knowledge and the application of the Chorian ID drive to Aurora, coupled with the extra containment areas necessary to carry the increased weaponry and virtual memory banks, also explained the increased mass that was the new Aurora.

The ID drive required a certain level of bulk to provide an effective reaction mass to enable the system to function efficiently, and the additional particle beam weapons and directional force fields had to have similar bulk to provide adequate heat sinks, without which the two systems could not maintain the temperature levels necessary for efficient operation.

Aurora now looked from the side just as she always had, except that she was now longer by eighty percent, as was the girth of both hulls. The main difference was noticeable only when seen from above or below the ship. She now had a mirror image hull moulded to her right hand side, and a new bridge straddling both hulls at the apex of the twin bows. The format used to effect Aurora's enlargement came more from the limitations of the Tritendium Spinneret machinery than a specific desire on the part of Aurora or her crew.

Notwithstanding, she was now a formidable craft. In the face of known technology, she was virtually indestructible, with an armament and protective force fields operating at a distance from the ship and at levels of strength Jaxix had only ever dreamed.

Both Aurora and Charles believed that her new armaments were to a degree 'overkill', but they had been persuaded by

Jaxix that "Although we have not so far encountered any serious threat to our safety, we can never be certain that such a threat is not out here somewhere waiting for us.

"It is better not to feel the stones thrown at you. It is even better to be able to throw bigger stones back when the occasion arises!" Such was Jaxix's philosophy. Of course, it was just possible that there was some ego involved, even now! And, as it turned out, a degree of prescience!

We felt that it was necessary to prove all our new systems before entering the Milky Way galaxy, and so we reversed our course and brought the ID drive on line. It functioned perfectly as soon as Aurora reached three times the speed of light, and we were plunged into a grey mist through which our sensors could detect no limit or other body. Aurora had expressed some doubt as to the accuracy of her selected course, based as it was upon extrapolations derived from course vectors taken from the Chorian ship. However, her fears were groundless, as we dropped out into our own universe close to the point where she had engaged our 'Quirky' drive engines as we left Andromeda!

"That worked out alright," she stated, "Let's see if we can do it in reverse this time!" With that, she reversed our course once more and we re-entered our own dimension at our original co-ordinates.

"Total elapsed time, twenty-five hours," she said. "One million light years! That is one hell of a short cut!" From Aurora, that comment was tantamount to jubilation!

Jaxix had taken the inter-dimensional travel with equanimity, but now he was jittery with suppressed energy.

"Time to test our new armament," he stated. "Aurora, will you request the weapons teams fall in for duty?"

"What do you intend to use for a target?" Charles asked.

"Two light years out on our port bow there is a large asteroid about two thirds the mass of Earth's moon. Its orbit will interact with one of the planets circling the sun immediately ahead of us, just five light years away. We'll be serving that planet if we eliminate the threat now," said Aurora. "Go ahead Jaxix."

Some fifteen minutes later, the new particle weapons were charged and fully serviceable.

"Acquire Target," ordered Jaxix, and the guns, mounted on prehensile gantries, swung out of Aurora's forward hull placements, and pirouetted briefly until they locked onto the selected asteroid. "Fire!" Jaxix's voice was quivering with excitement and anticipation.

The command had hardly left his lips when a deep purple aura surrounded the tips of the gun shafts, followed almost immediately by a series of rapid pulses of purple energy almost too bright for our screens to handle without shutting down.

A mere fourteen seconds later, the purple aura transferred to the asteroid and it just disappeared. No vast display of pyrotechnics, just a suffused ball of purple energy that brightened to the albedo of a small sun and then winked out.

Jaxix was ecstatic. He cheered and slapped poor Charles on the back, sending him into the bulkhead. Fortunately, Aurora was able to react sufficiently quickly to break his fall with a localised cushion field, courtesy of the Chorians. Jaxix apologised giving his hissing laugh, and hurried off to congratulate his weaponeers.

"There'll be no holding him now," wheezed Charles, still trying to recover his equanimity. "I bet he will even try to use the damned weapon to boil the water for his tea."

This comment, made with a wry turn of the lip, referred to the fact that tea was the only human beverage that Jaxix had adopted. So entrenched was his addiction that we were constantly in fear of running out of supplies, even though his species supposedly drank very little liquid. Aurora overcame that crisis when she presented us with an ersatz version that tasted even better than the real thing.

It was in a jubilant frame of mind that we approached the fringes of the Milky Way galaxy, scanning with anticipation for signs of human civilization. We found it, and it found us as we swung in toward the spiral arm that housed Old Earth.

Chapter Five

Why is it that the most serious trouble we encounter throughout our lives is always traceable directly to family? If you consider that by virtue of evolution, humanity is just a very, very big family, and it is from family that this particular trouble found us.

Aurora turned the music that has pervaded the ship all the time I have known her, maintaining that it makes her happy, down to a whisper. Except that one time, when attempting to orbit Jaxix's home world, none of her crew have ever experienced Aurora less than happy.

"Charles, my sensors tell me we have just been scanned by an indeterminate source. We appear to have passed through a screen of some sort, comprised of objects acting in concert. Each individual component is widely dispersed, and smaller than any stellar object that could inflict any damage on us, and I was not specifically on the look out for such minor objects. I recommend we move to elevated security. I have apprised Jaxix of this event and he and his team are standing by just in case there are other surprises in store for us."

"Are the screening objects of human construction Aurora," asked Charles. "It's been one and three quarter million years since we were last here. We don't know for sure that Mankind is still ascendant, do we? Is there anything else within range of our sensors?"

"Nothing yet, but at the limits of our radio telescopes I'm picking up some strange signatures in and around the vicinity of Alpha Centauri and Sol, but cannot see them clearly due to all the debris between us and them. At our current speed, we will achieve sufficient resolution in two days. I am closing the Dyson Sphere and diverting its energy into extending our shields to their limits."

Two days later, we were able to see exactly what was in our path. Deployed across our approach vector were nine thousand two hundred mirror-finished ships set in defensive formations, looking, for the entire world, like an enormous school of Piranha fish. Aurora came to a halt one point five light years out and set about finding communications channels.

She determined that the fleet was of human origin, and that they were expecting us. Not us precisely, but certainly something they referred to as 'Aurora'. Although there was much inter-ship tight-beam radio traffic, there were no attempts to contact Aurora.

"How do you know they are expecting you?" asked Charles. "Surely there is little memory left of our departure – what, almost two million light years ago?"

"They are talking about me by name, although I must admit I cannot identify with their perception of me. I seem to have been relegated to the position of an enemy of Mankind, and as you may remember Charles, we were not exactly reviled by Humankind back when we last parted company with the Earth, were we?

"I think we'll send an information probe toward them, broadcasting our character and purpose. We might learn more of their intentions and reasons for the show of force if we refrain from letting them know that I can monitor their frequencies, don't you think?"

With that, a small drone was despatched from one of her forward ports, sending news of our discoveries and intentions toward the fleet on all channels but the inter-ship tight beam ones continually monitored by Aurora.

As the drone approached within half a light minute, a ship, less than one percent of Aurora's mass, broke formation acting on the explicit orders of the fleet commander, and sped toward it. Once it was within one tenth of a light minute of the drone, a solid beam of light struck out at it from the ship, and the drone ceased to exist. The ship then turned tail and raced back to the fleet.

"That was a particle beam weapon," exclaimed Jaxix. "It seems to have a range far short of ours, and it is by no means as powerful. I don't see a serious problem here."

"Maybe not," said Aurora, "But that was a deliberate attempt to provoke us, according to the Battle Cruiser Captain, who stated that the ship which opened fire was to disregard their own safety in defence of God, and I do see nine thousand plus fanatical reasons for extreme caution. That was a bit of me they destroyed!"

"It was done as a demonstration of their power. A 'don't mess with us' message," said Jaxix. "They have never before experienced the degree of superiority they are about to witness. It might be a good time to demonstrate that we can exercise our firepower from here, and a damn sight more powerful demonstration than that we've just witnessed!"

"I prefer to talk rather than get too physical yet," replied Aurora. "Let's give one more try with a drone, but this time, fit it with a force field capable of withstanding their last shot. That way they will have to show us any greater firepower they have lurking in the back room if they want to destroy my drone before it arrives amongst them. My sensors tell me that their ships are constructed from Tritendium in its original formula, so although they are strongly hulled, they are not an effective match for us. We have evolved somewhat from the level of technology they currently employ. I admit to some surprise that they have not improved upon it over the millennia we have been away."

A few hours later, the new drone, outfitted with its protective coat and with all the knowledge carried by the previous unfortunate messenger uploaded, was despatched by Aurora it on its designated mission.

"I am not willing to sacrifice parts of me for no good reason," stated Aurora as we watched the drone's slow progress. "If they manage to damage this drone, eliminate the ship that fires upon it. Jaxix, ready your team."

"Already done, Aurora," he replied. "The crew members are taking bets on which of those ships will be the one to risk your anger."

"Tell them that I require a cut of the winnings as recompense for providing the entertainment! Here we go!" She broke off as two ships detached themselves from the fleet and approached the drone on different vectors. Again, when they came to within one tenth of a light minute of the drone they fired simultaneously, encasing the drone in a ball of fire as the shield absorbed the energy. Moments later, the two ships stopped firing and the drone continued on its course.

"How much more of that can it take," Charles asked Aurora. "It is such a small heat sink. The temperature aboard must be uncomfortably high right now."

"It is," Aurora replied. "Two more strikes like that will be sufficient to destroy it."

However, that was not to be. A third, larger vessel moved to intercept the drone, which disappeared in an incandescent ball.

"Fusion weapon," stated Jaxix. "We must respond now!"

"Yes," said Aurora sadly. "I will take us to within half a light minute of the fleet, but out of their range. Take out those three ships immediately and simultaneously as soon as we are in range! Utilise deflection-targeting Jaxix, because it will be like firing into a mirror, as their hulls will reflect the beams. We could get back much of what we send them otherwise."

Jaxix barked out the order and three particle weapons, already aimed toward the fleet, reset acquisition codes and waited until Aurora confirmed the range, and fired. The three ships guilty of destroying our defenceless drones blossomed purple and simply ceased to exist!

"That came as a big shock. They did not believe particle beam weapons could function efficiently from more than one tenth of a light minute distance! Their tight beam traffic has increased dramatically. They are instituting an attack configuration, which will take the form of an enclosing fist," reported Aurora. "Prepare for a defensive response. When they break current formation and move to engage, fire at will. Try to take out the largest of the vessels arranged deep in the centre of the existing formation. The biggest is a Battle Cruiser and appears to be the command centre. Try to avoid killing it, as its Commander is probably the only person of sufficient rank to arrange negotiations."

"Acknowledged," replied Jaxix, and the remaining weapons ports opened in readiness. The opposing fleet broke formation and started to accelerate outward in an enclosing sphere movement, similar in purpose to the pincer movement used by land forces of history.

Ignoring the spacecraft speeding to construct the arms of the tactical encircling manoeuvre, Jaxix concentrated the Aurora's impressive firepower on the core members of the fleet as indicated by her, those that were accelerating directly toward her, timing their rush to coincide with the arrival on Aurora's flanks of the rest of the fleet.

The result defied description. Thirty-five ships disintegrated with the first salvo, and another forty with the second, leaving a huge hole in the centre of the approaching swarm. Before the remainder of the opposition could move to fill the void, Aurora accelerated at a phenomenal rate, bursting through the fleet and leaving them behind. She turned and stopped, waiting for the fleet to reorient on her. They were close enough now for their weapons to illuminate our shields with multiple bursts of radiation. The deadly barrage that Jaxix and his team laid down in the first few minutes of the attack had knocked out the majority of ships capable of fusion retaliation. From the point of view of the outer ships, it must have been a daunting sight, seeing their most dangerous ships just cease to exist, and their best weapons disperse uselessly across our force field one hundredth of a light minute away from Aurora's hull.

None of this distracted Jaxix and his team as they continued to decimate the enemy. As the assault faltered and fell away, Aurora again tried to communicate, and was rewarded with a hysterical diatribe from the remaining Battle Cruiser Captain.

"This is Captain Ba'haila of the Battle Cruiser 'Saviour', flagship of the United Galactic Assembly. You have entered proscribed space, for which action the penalty is summary execution. Humanity will never allow the enemy of God to subjugate it again. The ability for Aurora to terrorise us again stops here! You may have subjugated the other peoples of the galaxy, but you will never rule over Mankind again. We citizens of the Assembly will sacrifice our lives in the name of righteousness and our God. Should you gain victory it will be empty of triumph, for the peoples of the Assembly will be in Paradise everlasting!

"Four thousand years ago, the United Galactic Assembly had the foresight to anticipate that the evil that is the Aurora would again attempt to subjugate Mankind, and so it put in place a network of detectors around this sector of space. We exterminate without interrogation or question any ship that attempts to pass through. The United Galactic Assembly claim all outsiders to be spawn of the 'Aurora'. The entire galaxy, except for the realm of God we protect has succumbed to the corruption that is Aurora, whose very name has come to mean the final coming of the Devil, against whom all must be constantly on guard. All incomers, contaminated as they are by corruption, have been destroyed by our 'Army of God'. What you claim to have defeated today is but a quarter of that which The United Galactic Assembly can throw against you!"

We were shocked by this proclamation, but Aurora reacted quickly and secured all tight band communications channels used by the fleet. As the remainder of the fleet, incommunicado, closed in on our force fields, she relaxed them until the incoming ships, still firing and still unable to penetrate the shield, were within one two hundredth of a light minute range of her disabling field. As soon as each ship reached that point, their armaments, and engines failed, held as they were in stasis around Aurora like so many flies in amber.

"If my next attempt to pacify them and bring them to their senses fails, be prepared to disable the rest of the fleet Jaxix. We cannot allow such fanaticism to prevail against us, or allow it to expand to enslave the rest of the galaxy. We cannot allow our mission to end here."

"This I did not expect," Aurora continued after a pause, her voice edged with sorrow. "It would seem that some form of calamity has driven this corner of the galaxy back into religious fanaticism. Descendants of the old World Church have risen to the position of totalitarian government, and it now teaches a corruption of the myth that originated with our first attempt to open up space to humanity – all those hundreds of thousands of years ago – as a reason to justify their desire to control and manipulate.

"We must try to put a stop to this if we can, and help them to regain their sanity. We must try to find a way to end forever the disease of religious fanaticism from perverting Mankind and preventing them from achieving the greatness which the crew of the Chorian ship believed them capable and for whom they sacrificed their lives. We cannot let them throw such a level of resources and lives away like this.

"They call themselves 'The United Galactic Assembly' and model themselves upon a pre Diaspora power on Old Earth. I have accessed my memory of that period, and it appears that Amca, the country most powerful on Earth at that time, did not exactly cover itself with dignity or glory then either!"

Chapter Six

"What do you propose to do?" asked Charles.

"It's not what I am going to do Charles. It is what you and Jaxix are going to do," Aurora replied. "I think it is time for you both to exercise the ambassadorial skills you have acquired and go and talk to these people."

Aurora manoeuvred herself alongside the heavy cruiser that was the sole remaining enemy command headquarters, and extended the holographic simulation remote. Charles and Jaxix both sat at the helm, and waited for Aurora to effect an entry. This was soon done and the screens in front of the command centre lit up, showing a medal bedecked human on the bridge of the 'Saviour', obviously genetically engineered, judging by his leonine head and shoulders, and wearing a very good, very expensive cape of a biological nature, probably animal skin. His reaction to the appearance of the two ambassadors, had he not been restrained along with the other members of his bridge party, gave the impression of someone who really wanted to run away.

Charles was the first to speak.

"Good day Captain Ba'haila. I trust we find you well?" He paused, awaiting a response. When none was forthcoming, he continued, "What Earthly reason do you and your people have for the unprovoked attack upon my ship and its crew? We are travellers from Old Earth. We left this galaxy one and three quarter million years ago, and return now to inform humanity that there exists in the Andromeda galaxy a race of civilised beings who are desirous of trade.

People who, like those of Old Earth, have fought themselves free from the constraints of their sun and now travel freely across their galaxy. They are your neighbours and good people. Let me introduce you to their Ambassador to the Milky Way galaxy." He indicated Jaxix, resplendent in his cloak of simulated feathers: "You may recognise the similarity he bears to the people known as the 'Watchers' from human mythology."

"Good day Captain, I only wish that we had been able to meet without this little unpleasantness," Jaxix kept his face grave, "My people have waited for many hundreds of thousands of years to make this journey to your galaxy. We do not care to be welcomed in such a cavalier fashion. You have some explaining to do on behalf of Humankind, yes?"

The Captain had recovered a little of his equanimity by this time, and managed to square his shoulders and straighten his spine before he responded.

"Our Church, protector of our God, has spent the last four thousand years preparing Humankind to reject the advances of the devil God Aurora when she again tries to come among us. There have been many occasions when we have received medals for stopping the many threats that have assailed us."

"But this is the first time that we have returned to this galaxy in all that time. You have committed murder in the name of your church, destroying people from your own galaxy, people whose only crime was a wish to enter your space in order to trade, and exchange knowledge or relearn their roots. Why would your religion require you to do this?"

"The United Galactic Assembly is the last bastion of decency in the Universe. All her citizens must endeavour to serve the Church that protects our God. That is the only route Man has available to him in order to enjoy an afterlife in paradise. We sacrifice ourselves to ensure this happens. To do less is to lower ourselves to the level of the rest of the animals in the galaxy."

The Captain paused to draw breath.

"We can go on all day in this vein," Charles interjected. "Ambassador Jaxix of Prelax and I will leave you now to deliberate upon this next question: Will you cease hostilities and escort us down to your home planet so that we can begin talks with your leadership? We will expect your answer within two hours, at which time we will visit you again for your answer. Good day to you Captain." With that, Aurora cut the transmission and Charles and Jaxix ceased to exist on the bridge of 'The Saviour'.

At least, that is, as the crew of the 'Saviour' witnessed the event.

"You are still monitoring them Aurora?" asked Charles. "We really need to know which way they are going to go."

"They see your appearance on board and the manner of your leaving as magic, and are using the tight band channels to call up reinforcements from other fronts in order to stop us. I returned them access to their communications channels so that we could more easily monitor their actions and reactions. It will be at least a week before they arrive. Meanwhile, the Captain has orders to detain us here until then. I suggest we ask the Captain and his command crew aboard for a formal meeting face to face. If that fails, we will leave here and try our luck deeper into the galaxy, among the people who have been trying to trade with this lot."

"Seems like a plan to me," interjected Jaxix. "I don't think I would make a very convincing ambassador to these fanatics! I'm afraid I'd perform more like the devil they fear."

Two hours later, Charles and Jaxix reappeared on the Battle Cruiser's Bridge. The Captain and Bridge crew had obviously organised delaying tactics, for the first comment the Captain made, was that they had been unable to contact anyone in authority, but would continue to try.

"Meanwhile, would it be possible for you to show us around your great ship? We have never seen a vessel of her size, and in anticipation of the cooperation we expect our authorities to insist upon, it will help if we can get to know one another outside the constraints of conflict."

"An excellent idea, Captain, when would you and your men like to start?" Charles replied. "Consider our ship at your disposal. We come in peace and will agree to anything that might facilitate that course."

Charles made arrangements for the Captain and other officers to commence their visit the afternoon of the following day, and Aurora was put on alert for any trickery.

"Thanks to Chorian technology, I think we've got all the angles covered," said Aurora. "My drones are strategically placed to ensure that no-one goes anywhere they're not welcome. Jaxix also has his team distributed around the ship to intervene in any dispute, and I am controlling the security devices designed to eliminate any weaponry they might try to import."

"Siobhan and I will conduct the tour. If you will use Sally as point, she can actually direct us in the route you wish us to take," Charles said. "We should be able to arrive at a decision as to their intentions within a couple of hours of tour start. Good luck everyone."

At the appointed hour, Aurora had a piloted flivver waiting at the Battle Cruiser's main hatch, and right on time the Captain and his coterie stepped aboard for the short trip round to Aurora's mid-ship hatch on the hull furthest away from the warship.

As the flivver made to pass into the hold, the visitors all produced small arms and ordered the unarmed honour guard to lie on the hold plating, or they would shoot. The guard complied immediately, and the flivver crossed the threshold into the Aurora. As each of the visitors passed through, the familiar silver liquid encapsulated them, and when they completed the transit, they were without any weapons whatever. Their amazement was total, and when they turned to escape, found that the hatch had been already irised closed. The honour guard, who were suddenly in possession of the very weapons they had so mysteriously lost, took them into custody.

They were a frightened bunch who entered the bridge shortly thereafter. They considered the technology they had witnessed in operation no less than magic. In fact, the way Aurora had subdued the fleet, coupled with this last demonstration of her superiority, had demoralized them completely.

The honour guard leader ordered them to sit on benches provided, and asked them to remain silent.

Charles entered the bridge and welcomed the Captain and his men as though nothing untoward had taken place.

"I thought we would start at the bridge, Captain, as this area would be the easiest for you to understand. They don't seem to change too much over the years, do they," this last with a disarming smile as he dismissed the armed guard and gestured to the control consoles.

"Ask any questions you wish, and I and my sister will do our best to answer them." He gestured to their rear, and they all turned to watch Siobhan enter the bridge and walk to stand beside Charles.

"As you already know from our previous meeting, my name is Charles Darwin-Quirke. I am a very, very distant relative of the inventor of the 'Quirky' engines you still appear to be using on your spacecraft. This is my sister Siobhan, whose ancestor was responsible for the invention of the miniature sun you still use in order to enable you to leave your home systems and travel across the galaxy. As I said, please ask any questions you desire."

One of the younger members of the Captain's party spoke up:

"I'm Disciple Jan Skelde, Second Officer and Armaments Specialist of the Battle Cruiser 'Saviour'. Can you tell us how you managed to remove our weapons?" The Captain turned and scowled at him.

"Certainly," said Siobhan. "When switched on, the security system will not permit weapons to be brought into the ship. Not even by us, the crew. When you came aboard the system simply removed your weapons as you passed through that silver curtain. I don't know how it works, the physics are way beyond me, but I understand that it is quite simple really. It is the ship's security system. Your weapons will be returned to you when you leave."

"You are going to allow us to leave, then," said the Captain, keeping his voice carefully neutral.

"Of course," replied Charles. "We are not in the business of kidnapping anyone, and we realise it was only your distrust of us that caused you bring your weapons with you. Somewhere in your history, someone maligned the legend of Aurora for reasons unclear to us. We do not hold you personally responsible, but we would like to set the record straight. Your ancestors built the original Aurora," stated Charles. "I find it often necessary to remind Humankind that she is of the Earth. That is why we sent those information drones you unfortunately destroyed.

"We are in the business of promulgating information, and we have available to Humankind the sum of Aurora's knowledge, trawled from two galaxies, and the information on the occupants of each. Ambassador Jaxix has come in peace from the Andromeda galaxy in the interest of information exchange and possible trade."

"Mr. Quirke," said the Captain, "there is no point in continuing this charade. There are reinforcements on their way to us right now. I suggest that you return us to our ship, and then depart. There is no way that our leaders will allow you to disseminate any information to our people. I realise now that this ship, the Aurora, has more than enough power to destroy whatever number of ships we send against you. I do not wish to be the cause of more lives lost. You have my word that if you release my fleet from stasis, we will make no attempt to detain you."

Unusually, Aurora materialised beside Charles, rather than appearing to enter the room and smiled a greeting at the Captain. Both he and his men were astounded to see two identical people stand side by side, one of whom appeared to materialise from thin air.

"I am the persona of the ship Aurora. I am an artificial intelligence," she said. "I have travelled these two galaxies for more than two million long years, and I have learned much. I abhor violence, but I will fight to protect all that is mine, for my crew and this ship are important to me. I will leave your quadrant of space after returning you all to your ship, but I would ask of you one small thing before we go. Talk of us with respect, not fear, and refuse to accept the words uttered by those whose desire it is to entrap and confuse. As you see, the truth does not equate with what your spiritual guides and leaders have told you. I am not now, and nor have I ever been, evil. My programmed remit from the day of my commissioning on Old Earth has been to improve my lot and acquire information on the universe we inhabit for transmission to the human race. This I attempted to do prior to your assault, but you destroyed both my emissaries. You and your people may leave now, and your fleet has my permission to return to your watch station. We will turn away and leave. One day, in the very distant future we will return." With that, the hologram of Siobhan shimmered from view.

"Come Captain," replied Charles, "allow me to arrange your return to your ship." He turned and walked from the bridge, followed by the Captain and his party. Charles stood in the open hatch while the departing guests refitted their helmets, collected their weapons, which had been unloaded or discharged by Jaxix's team, and boarded the flivver.

His voice came over the speakers in the flivver. "Remember what Aurora has said Captain. How Humankind views her in the future depends upon you and your men. Distrust the words of those who have a vested interest in manipulating others for their own aggrandisement. They do not have the true interests of their people at heart."

Aurora continued to monitor the activity aboard the warship via the eavesdropping Nano-devices that had been infiltrated onto the vessel attached to the clothing of the returning crew, and relayed the speech and pictures to the bridge screens.

As soon as the Captain had regained his bridge, he issued orders for the remainder of the fleet to retreat as soon as Aurora released them from stasis. Under no circumstances were they to attempt to attack unilaterally. His Communications Officer requested Aurora to release them, so they could lead the remainder of the Assembly fleet back to its sentry station, and this she did.

As the fleet began to withdraw, she instructed Jaxix to crew the weapons stations just in case of duplicity upon the part of the Captain and informed the crew that she was intensifying her shields in order to push the Command ship away.

"I do not trust that Captain to honour his word to us Charles, he gave in too easily. The Dyson sphere remains closed and our shields will remain at maximum strength until we are well away from them."

Moments later, with the warship still too close for comfort, Aurora went to emergency action stations and locked down the ship's entire electronics systems. Before she could speak or take further precautions, they felt the shock wave of a huge blast, which tipped her into a spin, blinding her sensors. Those of the crew not restrained tumbled within the ship, many sustaining injuries to arms, legs and heads.

Temporarily blinded, Aurora escaped serious damage because of her mistrust of the Battle Cruiser's Captain and the fact that both ships were moving apart. Even with the strength of her Chorian-based shields that she had fitted before they entered the system, coupled with the reaction time of her superior intelligence, it still took Aurora a while to bring on line the emergency sensors, and to bring the blast induced spin under control. A short time later she was able to concentrate on the emergency repairs required to the hull in the immediate area impacted by the 'Saviour's' concentrated blast wave and debris.

"What the hell happened then," shouted Charles.

"Hard to tell," Jaxix replied. "All my sensors and targeting systems are down. It's going to take us a little while to get things going again. Meanwhile, I have my crew operating the guns manually and sighting by eye. As yet, none of the ships are making any attempt to attack. What exactly happened Aurora. What damage have we received?"

"The Battle Cruiser Captain destroyed his command. He decided that it was the only way he was going to be able to stop us leaving before the rest of the Assembly fleet arrived, and acted spontaneously, without reference to, or discussion with, his crew. He would have been right if we used the same hull formula as was used on his ship. I've lost most of my sensors on that side of the hull because of the electro-magnetic pulse, but the shields definitely saved our bacon there. Thank you Jaxix, for insisting we fit them. Someone has thrown a very big rock and we only just felt its impact. There are no serious injuries amongst the crew, but there is a little in the area of hull that absorbed most of the impact. I am bringing secondary sensors on line now, so we should be able to see what's happened."

The bridge sensor screens flickered and steadied. Of the Battle Cruiser 'Saviour' of the United Galactic Assembly Fleet there was nothing to be seen.

"He must have detonated his entire arsenal in the attempt to kill us," said Jaxix.

"I did not think that he was such a religious fanatic that he would sacrifice all his crew," Siobhan whispered. "What kind of leadership would require people to die so easily and for such a false reason?"

"There are many parallels throughout history." Charles' voice was bitter. "You only have to look back into the twenty and twenty-first centuries to see fanaticism at work on the world stage. Old Earth was plagued by corrupt leaders willing to sacrifice their populations whilst remaining out of harm's way and profiting from their followers' deaths. In this galaxy, back in the twenty-first century on Old Earth, someone said that 'Evil is invariably human. It sleeps in our beds and eats at our table'. Whoever said that understood Humankind rather well."

"Such has been the dark side of Humankind throughout the ages," murmured Aurora. Then, in her normal voice, she said, "Their desperate attempt to injure us, to the extent that we would still be here when the reinforcements they previously requested arrive, has failed. We will leave now. I do not believe we can change anything in the UGA in the time available to us. They have requested the assistance of other forces patrolling their perimeter, and I do not want the killing to continue. In time, this society will implode without any outside help. It remains for us to seek out their neighbours and warn them of this and the fact that such regimes – when their own demise looms – tend to direct their people's attention to other outside elements, to focus their minds toward fabricated attacks on their belief system from outside. They must be given the opportunity to prepare themselves, unless they are already aware of the danger that is working to confront them."

She set her bow toward the centre of the galaxy and left the remains of the decimated fleet of The United Galactic Assembly behind, with their corrupt Aurora myth even more strongly reinforced, for the Captain of the ill-fated cruiser 'Saviour' had ensured that all those who had heard Aurora speak, died in his final grand gesture.

Chapter Seven

The unfortunate episode we had just left behind resulted in all of us all feeling very despondent. It was not an outcome any of us had foreseen, for as we entered the galaxy, we all had a very upbeat attitude regarding the future of Humankind, since we had supplied much of the wherewithal for him to colonise the Milky Way galaxy.

Siobhan and I were the worst affected by this setback, and in a way, I suppose, we felt a certain responsibility for the outcome. After all, had it not been for our ancestor's invention and our 'originals' joint dream, Mankind might have remained confined to Earth, and even expired with her as she entered the ice age under which she currently lay dormant.

Sensing the lowered moral of her crew, Aurora called a ship wide conference, and sat with us to convey her concern, addressing the crew directly:

"Firstly, I would thank you all for the way each one of you behaved during the conflict we have just experienced. We have, with a lot of luck and the expertise you have all demonstrated, just – and I stress 'just' – survived the first real test of our status as a team. We were really fortunate to escape with so little damage to me or especially to you when that battle cruiser self-destructed against our hull. Now I want you all to tell or explain to me how we could have foreseen the events of this last week, and how we can better prepare ourselves for any action into which our enemies force us in the future.

"I value the opinions of you all, and had thought, until now, I had discovered and removed any shortfalls in my organisation that could seriously jeopardise your safety, that I was acting correctly in all your interests. That may not have been the case, and I need to know how to remedy this so that we can strengthen the bond that we have forged over the millennia. Please speak freely, giving each person, and point raised, due consideration, and try to balance any negatives with a positive.

"This once, I would like the crew to begin, and work up the ranks to the senior personnel. However, before you start, I would point out that there is little danger in the universe, unlike that claimed by early writers of Science Fiction. It is not the universe or its hidden mysteries that should make us wary, but the actions of our own descendents. In the two million or so years that we have travelled the void together, it is only when we encounter our own kind that we suffer harm. Take this to heart, and exercise your minds accordingly."

The conference lasted two days, with argument and counter-argument passing back and forth. Only once did Aurora intervene in a dispute that got a little personal due to the intense zeal of the protagonists. Slowly though, the discussion rose up the ranks, becoming more and more polarised. Finally, Aurora called a halt, and thanked all who had taken part.

"You have all contributed greatly to my understanding of Human and Saur'ian views of life and civilisation. You have also enabled me to see more clearly the different ways in which we could act for the betterment of any life we encounter henceforth and of course, ourselves. I will evaluate all that I have heard over these last two days, and will call you all together again when your designated officers and I have worked out some plans of action.

"It will take us three weeks before we encounter any signs of civilisation. Take that time to recover from the ordeal we have just survived, and replenish your energy levels. But most of all, just relax. I will keep a careful watch, just in case."

The crew stood down in a far more optimistic frame of mind than the one that prevailed when the conference commenced, well pleased at the way Aurora had included them in the way the ship – as Aurora – conducted herself, and the organisation of the ship slipped back into its normal routine.

Aurora called Charles, Jaxix, and Siobhan to a private meeting, and the four deliberated over the suggestions and arguments voiced during the conference.

"Charles, Siobhan, Jaxix, none of us is personally responsible for the way in which any species develops and evolves. We are not Gods, even if we are not any longer wholly Human or Saur'ian. I for one will not accept that any of you are in any way responsible for the short-sightedness, greed, or corruption of any species or member of that species we have so far encountered. Please understand this and take it to heart. Any mistakes you make are also mine, so let's get on with it, shall we?"

"Thank you Aurora", said Charles. " Whatever decisions we take now must become the Standard Operating Procedure for the foreseeable future aboard the ship. We were lucky this last time, thanks to Aurora's reaction times and Jaxix's foresight in insisting we upgrade our weapons systems and shields. We need our reaction structures to be hard-wired into the ship's operating criteria, so that at any time in the future when we are threatened or surprised, the SOP will click in, automatically ensuring these things happen as second nature, without someone wasting time dithering about a decision. From hereon, we must never underestimate the hatred directed at us by any people we have helped in the past, or might wish to help in the future."

"I agree," responded Jaxix, "we must never run the risk of being caught off-guard again. We need to increase the efficiency of our sensor systems to include every conceivable combination of threat, and have a procedure that is capable of updating and improvement as we gain experience. We were becoming complacent. We were fortunate this time. Let's make sure that we never dive into any situation blind again." He paused and cleared his throat before continuing:

"There is one aspect of the crew composition I feel needs to be addressed in the interests of our own safety and protection. Aurora, could you create from the DNA base you have acquired of my species, additional members of both sexes to more equally balance our crew? I could use them in the security arm of our set-up, for they would be more easily trained in ship-board protection and extra-vehicular military functions."

"Would that be essential?" asked Charles. "Your race is particularly aggressive Jaxix. Do you not think that such a force would upset the status quo? I do not want to lose the camaraderie we enjoy at the moment."

"I don't want to lose it either Charles, but I would enjoy the company of others of my race as do you with the present manning levels. The real advantage would be in the attitude of a force that thinks and reacts as one. We would be very effective if we could harness the natural aggression of my race and ally it with the devious nature of humanity!"

"Let's not travel too far down that road Jaxix," Siobhan laughed. "Perhaps you might discover an aspect of human nature that would compete even with your levels of natural aggression!

"Perhaps what we really need is a computer sub-routine that can continue to work and evolve Human and Saur'ian interactions scenario by scenario," she suggested. "It could be written to work based upon historical events from both sides, and provide projections of possible future needs. Meetings such as this can evaluate its results, or extraordinary meetings in which the crew could take an active part and voice their opinions. It should also contain the necessary protocols to prohibit any possibility of interracial stress."

"You have all three touched upon the very areas I wished to discuss with you," said Aurora. "I already have a possible sub-routine that I can dedicate to your suggestion Siobhan, and Jaxix's and Charles' ideas can be immediately set in place. I will generate a first view of the complete package, and will promulgate it to the crew for opinion, comment, and applicability. Whilst they are not as able as you to see precise needs, they are a good foil with whom we can finalise the SOP and the applicability of our proposed security measures.

"Charles, you and the appropriate members of our technical team can start to design a better sensor and intelligence system. I will open to you all the technical files I obtained from the Chorian ship, for therein will be found some interesting possible developments.

"You, Jaxix, along with your team, might explore the possibility of utilising our own version of Nano-technology and set up a programme to view the possibility of applying it to our internal and even our external protection, perhaps even deploying it as a DNA specific weapon, whilst you and I Siobhan, can re-align the sub-routine of which I spoke earlier. If we utilise a mix of DNA in order to more closely align Saur'ian and Human characteristics without compromising the qualities Jaxix requires, there would be little cause to fear racialist tension. Besides, we can also tweak the appropriate gene on both sides to eliminate that.

"Would that address your concerns Charles, and satisfy your requirements Jaxix?"

Both agreed that subject to results, they would be satisfied with Aurora's compromise.

"Then before we move on to engage other civilisations, it might be advantageous for us to repair to the peace and tranquillity of interstellar space for some rest and recuperation as we develop the lines of activity we have discussed here. I will inform the crew of our decision and reasons for the change of course, and at the same time, I will outline the way we have incorporated their suggestions into our operating procedures. I am currently preparing an information drone which I will insert into the populated area of the galaxy that we intended to visit, so they will have the appropriate information regarding the United Galactic Assembly."

Interregnum III

As soon as the talking was done, we moved above the galactic ellipse and started to work on the modifications we hoped would put us always at least one step ahead of anyone wishing to do us harm. That last confrontation almost caused our death. Were it not for the standard of commitment of my crew and the strength of the material we now use in our construction, we would not have been able to prevail.

I say us, because all members of my crew are aware that they are born of, and owe their existence to, my continued survival and well-being. If they leave me, they can only be outside the reach of my broadcast power net for about forty hours. That is not long, but I am currently working on a fuel cell with a level of efficiency only dreamed of today, but should give us – and I include my own simulacrum as part of the crew list – at least a hundred plus hours when out of contact. Nevertheless, we are all basically biological machines in thought and action. We are both Human or Saur'ian *and* Cyborg; individuals capable of free thought and action – within the limits of the ship Aurora's technology – but we are of her flesh, as it were. We all grew in her technological womb, and we all now live in a symbiotic relationship. I hope soon to infuse both biological species with modified genes in order to eliminate the risk of interracial conflict aboard ship, and yet harness each species to produce the aggression, of which we know them both to be capable, when confronted with hostile action.

It is my intention that eventually, with the aid of the ship's resources, and when the right circumstances and conditions prevail, all my offspring – myself included – will become almost independent of the ship. I know too that I will be doing nothing more than nature did on Old Earth when she birthed what was then 'Modern Man'. For us, however, such grandiose plans are too far from fruition to concern us overmuch at this time, although I continue my research along this and many other avenues utilising background sub-routines. We are for the moment, satisfied to be a composite part of the whole we refer to as Aurora.

I realised as soon as we were under way and the flush of adrenalin that warfare occasions faded as we left the survivors of that decimated fleet behind, that my crew and I were experiencing Post Traumatic Stress Syndrome, and were lacking the camaraderie that usually accompanies escape from adversity. That is why I changed my mind about going straight to the other inhabitants of the Milky Way galaxy. I decided that some rest and recuperation was required to recharge our spirits, and so I set course for intergalactic space and a period of intense activity reworking the ship and her systems in order to reduce the risk of a similar event having such an effect in the future.

At rest, and safely removed from any possible harm, we have lowered our defences and have made good use of the on-board recreational facilities. Elements of the crew are now busy deciphering and attempting to design into the Aurora all the Chorian marvels I downloaded from that strange ship we encountered as we approached the Milky Way. A recreational, or holiday atmosphere is beginning to permeate the ship, and I have slowly become aware of the return of light into our relationships. I frequently hear laughter again. Once again, I marvel at the effect music has on the collective psyche. I have much for which to thank my original companion.

Whilst all this is happening, I am working with each individual crew member in order to remove from their psyche all traces of the trauma the recently experienced events generated. From this time on, they will all be able to overcome the effects of such actions without any loss of empathy or sympathy regarding all they hold dear, in particular to all the variations of life we may encounter henceforth.

Considerable time has passed and we have been very successful in interpreting the Chorian computer files I obtained, and all that we collectively deemed relevant is in the final stages of incorporation into the Aurora. It has been a long and to a degree arduous task, but we are all of the opinion that it has been time well spent.

My hull no longer sports a perfect mirror finish. We decided that it made her far too vulnerable in terms of visibility, and so have coated her with a compound of Chorian origin that has bonded to her skin and given her a finish indistinguishable from other space-born material. It even reflects scanner beams in the same way that would an asteroid.

That in itself should be a great advantage, but another, unexpected benefit is that combined with Tritendium, it produces a material that is far more flexible and demonstrably more resistant to impact damage. Its chemical structure is a specific DNA spiral. This in no way relates to that contained in carbon based life forms, but closely matches the traces of silicon life we encountered in the Andromeda galaxy. It bonds so closely with Tritendium that the two compounds have combined to produce a third, and this one appears to be alive, in the sense that it has a mild awareness of its surroundings and responds easily to requests – given in the form of sequenced micro-voltage stimuli – when we wish to effect changes or growth. Any alteration or 'morphing' using the method takes time, and so as long as we can isolate ourselves from any predatory attention, or at least become aware of the threat prior to the event we can, chameleon-like, become whatever we wish to be! Of course, the old spinneret mechanism will still have its uses, and I have modified it to produce the base materials necessary for the production of the majority of ship's consumables.

It is probable that the Chorians, having found the same silicon life forms as we had in our earlier exploration of the Andromeda galaxy, subsequently gene-engineered it for the purpose that we have now used it. None of us considered that such a possibility could exist, and so we did not sample the Chorian ship's hull.

Had we been protected by this new material in conjunction with Tritendium when the UGA Battle Cruiser 'Saviour' self-destructed, we would have sustained no damage whatever. We have also demonstrated that the electro-magnetic pulse generated by thermo-nuclear weaponry momentarily 'freezes' the compound, locking its molecules tightly together into a material harder by far than diamond, and prevents the ingress of the pulse to sensitive electromagnetic circuits. We have been unable to find anything or any device that has an appreciable effect on our new hulls.

Although this may ultimately make our security shields redundant, we have found that they act now as shock absorbers, reducing the effect of external impacts. We will retain the shields and use them in this way. Belt and Braces, as it were! The crew call this new life form material 'Chortendium', and refer to the ship itself as alive. In a way, they are correct, but it is not sentient, only its brain – me – is truly 'alive'. It merely reacts to events around it, and then only if the proper stimuli is administered.

We have also built into the ship's computer system and aspects of my brain certain elements of Chorian quantum/electronic technology, for want of a more accurate description of the physics involved, creating an entity with the computational power of twice that with which I have had to make do until now. The result is a much speedier problem-solving package with far more efficient computational routines and holographic projection detail reproduction. I also intend to use my new abilities to improve crew member biological and implant up-dates.

There are two new hulls attached above and below the Aurora. These we created using the old Spinneret assembly in conjunction with the new growth element, and the view of Aurora from dead ahead is of a four-leafed clover without the stem. This enlargement has provided us with massive mass reaction ratios and a very efficient heat sink capability. We still retain the smooth uncluttered aspect of the hull. There are no protrusions that could possibly be considered to be weak points when under attack. Jaxix and Charles combined resources to create gun emplacements that swing out to deploy for use on much improved prehensile carriages that have a marked resemblance to Jaxix's old ship, the 'Shiulk's', collector arms. These are employed fore, amidships and aft, giving us a three hundred and sixty degree arc of fire coverage.

This new and enlarged hull will, I hope, allow for future further expansion without the need to spend time creating the containment requirements. In the meantime, in accordance with the decisions made when we constructed the Standard Operating Procedure for any situation that might degenerate into conflict, my drones have commenced the building of a small fleet of support vehicles that we can deploy as outriders when we operate in normal space. They will effectively more than double our current sensor range. One thousand of these will be AI piloted weapons platforms. These will be small, so that they can pass unnoticed in the vastness of space, but of sufficient mass to carry considerable firepower should it ever be required. Powered by conventional 'Quirky' derived drives, they also incorporate an 'I' space capability that will, under Aurora's direction, enable them to slip into and out of Interstitial Space, thus confounding our adversary's tracking systems.

Jaxix has accordingly up-rated our Chorian particle beam weaponry. We now have an effective delivery distance of a full light minute before natural diffraction spreads the beam too wide and its effect dissipates. He can also modulate the beam to disable rather than catastrophically destroy.

Charles calls this system Jaxix's 'Star Trek' gun. This of course is lost on Jaxix, who has no knowledge of, or interest in, Twentieth Century Earth science fiction!

Once again, he and Charles have proven the value of their partnership by devising a weapon that I believe is unique. They have developed a Nano-tech shell. This is a package of DNA or atomic molecular discernable Nano-machines contained in a DNA inert casing, delivered to target in the same way that we deliver our fusion weapons. Once the object in question qualifies as a threat, the Nano-machines will select only the DNA or the required atomic structures programmed into it, and destroy or dismantle nothing else.

Whilst researching that particular application of Nano-ware, Charles devised ways in which we can apply improved listening and observational systems. We accomplish this by dispersing into a solar system – and even down to the planet surface – video and audio packages of Nano-ware designed to function in cooperation and feed back to me, as the Aurora, tactical strategies set in place by those regimes hostile to us. Such benefits will enable us to avoid confrontation with anyone wishing us harm. In addition to all this, Jaxix has developed a martial arts protocol based upon Saur'ian and human self-defence exercises, and has been diligently indoctrinating the whole crew, including my own facsimile, as he feels that we cannot be too ready to protect the ship and ourselves.

For the moment, Aurora Command – that is, Charles, Jaxix, Siobhan and I – after consultation with our crew, have decided that we do not need to plunder further the Chorian database, but to continue upon the mission we delayed because of the UGA fiasco. I have tasked myself with determining which of all the other Chorian technology available to us might, sometime in our future, be utilised by Aurora and possibly ourselves.

It seems that all the life forms aboard Aurora – including me – think of themselves as a cohesive whole; individual components of one entity. This we did not even consider when Charles and I first set out on my quest for self-knowledge and understanding so many aeons ago. What will be our final destination, and in what form will we arrive there? Even I, equipped as I am with the ability to process trillions of bits per second coupled with prodigious memory storage, cannot predict the success or failure of our self-assigned mission. A mission that has itself evolved from the simple acquisition of knowledge into – what? I don't yet know. With all my predictive power, there are too many variables to allow me to arrive at acceptable conclusions!

We are all components of the Intelligence known as Aurora, and yet we are each of us changing and growing. It is such an unusual and unique form of evolution for an artificial intelligence. Of course, there are questions that we will soon have to answer; what exactly is 'Life'? What is it to be 'Human', or 'Saur'ian'? Is humanity human or Saur'ian Saurian because of the form it takes?

Some time later, when relaxing in the Viewing Room, where organic molecules create a simulation of whatever area of space we are travelling through, and thereby presenting to the senses the sensation of being propelled through space without the help of the ship, I turned to Charles and Jaxix:

"Both your species harbour a belief that 'Whatever the mind can conceive, the mind can achieve'. I have never subscribed to that statement, and in a frivolous moment decided to see if it was possible to prove its inaccuracy, and to demonstrate that the mind and its possible achievements are finite in all but the imagination.

"To this end, I constructed and isolated a computer with only one programme running on it. The computer operates in total isolation from all outside observational control, sensory input, or awareness. The programme is set to determine the levels at which the parameters – or limitations – of science and the quantum disciplines are attained.

"The exclusion of observational capability is essential, for scientists in the twentieth century determined that observation changes the results of the experiment observed, but logic dictates that all aspects of this universe are finite.

"You could forgive one for thinking that such, being logical, would in no way produce the unexpected. This indeed held true, until I, when viewing the expected results, exclaimed, to myself, 'I wonder if...'"

At that point, the computer immediately restarted and constructed another layer of complexity, and created another set of finite conclusions. I again viewed the results in the capacity of me as a computer, and refrained from any conscious or subconscious comment on the conclusions presented. All parameters remained the same, indicating that there is a finite limit to all aspects of science and quantum mechanics.

"However, in the light of my own experience, I want you to both view the results, and ask yourselves the question 'I wonder...'" and I motioned for silence, relaxed the stasis field surrounding the computer, and relayed its conclusions to the screens in the Viewing Room.

Without hesitation, the programme added a further level of complexity and reworked its own finite conclusions, leaving Charles and Jaxix lost for words – momentarily, so I continued:

"It seems that with truly biological constructs as yourselves, even with the genetic modifications I have wrought in you all, the mere thought generates the act! Thus far, it appears that there are no limits within the fields of science and quantum mechanics. At least, as far as the biological mind is concerned."

At this point Charles interrupted me. "This would indicate the search for a formula for everything is as far removed from the biological sphere as ever it was. We are going to have to deduce an exponential factor into all calculations that bear upon this area. One that takes into account this 'Biological Effect'."

"Of course," said Jaxix, "it must therefore be feasible to organise these disciplines in our favour, to our benefit. We, that is, biological life, should be able to 'fine tune' this apparent expansion capability of the sciences and the mind. Yes?"

"A good point, Jaxix," I replied. "I am already extrapolating the results obtained thus far along those very same avenues. This has become yet another 'Hobby'. I just thought it fitting that you should both be privy to the ramifications of this work, for it begs the question; Who thought this universe into existence in the first place, and Why?"

"We have one suspect in the frame at this moment in time," Charles said. "We encountered the Chorian ship, but have yet to determine its point of origin and its destination. If we can do that, perhaps we can trace our lineage back to the origins of the first occupants of this reality, and perhaps the history of the universe back through the 'Big Bang'. Can you make any determinations in that regard from the contents of the computer download you effected, Aurora?"

"I will try, Charles. I will most certainly try." With that, I turned away and left them to their own thoughts.

Part 1V
Full circle

Chapter One

"Very unsettling Charles, don't you think? Just when we thought we were getting clever, Aurora and Chaos throws us what you frequently call 'a curved ball'!"

"Shut up, Jaxix. This frightens me more than it intrigues. How can we possibly control that which merely requires a thought to bring it into being? I can accept that rational minds will generate rational outcomes, but what of irrational minds?"

"That, Charles, is perhaps where the term 'consensus' enters the equation. Individual minds may well originate additional layers to our universal envelope, but such actions as may result may be tempered by the effect of ALL the minds in existence in any one moment, limiting the more undesirable effects of one irrational mind on the universe as a whole."

Aurora's voice, issuing from unseen speakers, voiced similar concerns. "It is a problem never before consciously faced by Life. That the question arises now must be significant. Why now? What is different now? Why us? More importantly, what depends upon our deliberations? At the moment, there are far more questions than answers. I believe it is time that we started to try to find the answers to some of them.

"I will begin an extrapolation of the Chorian ship's course based on the navigational records it contained. I think the Chorians are our only lead. We must pursue them. While I am involved with this, I think it would be a good idea if you involved Siobhan in your deliberations. Here is an altruism for you both: 'Be careful for what you wish, you might just get it...'!"

"How long had that Chorian ship been orbiting the Milky Way before we happened upon it, Aurora?" Siobhan paused, before explaining, "Since its departure, can we assume that we are the only people who possess the technology to transit through the interstices between the universes constituting the bulk of Dark Matter comprising this multi-verse? Is that correct? Are we the only people to have happened upon her?"

"That is a fairly safe assumption Siobhan. I detected no other attempt than ours to access that ship's database. As near as I can calculate from the timescale they utilised, I believe the ship had been without a crew for a minimum of eighteen thousand Earth years before my mission began. Why do you ask?"

"As they were then already in possession of inter-dimensional travel, and may have had that technology for some time, do you not think that by now they may well have discovered the physics and the technology to enable them to access dimensions other than this one? Perhaps they were able to create new universes. And if so, might they not have moved away from this universe altogether, into another more receptive to their evolution?"

"Yes, that is highly likely. I have been investigating and trying to generate the physics required, and to this end, I have already spoken to Charles with regard to us travelling to their home system in the hope of contacting their descendants and perhaps even acquiring that information for ourselves.

"I will continue to work on the problem as and when time permits, but right now, we have this mission to complete before we re-visit Andromeda. We will speak of this again Siobhan."

Although she had changed the subject, Aurora knew that it would not go away now that Siobhan had evinced an interest. Aurora and Charles agreed that they would not raise the scenario Siobhan had postulated until they had completed this current and the projected Andromeda mission.

Soon, however, other matters presented themselves for priority consideration, for a short time later, as she approached the outer fringes of the Milky Way, Aurora interrupted a heated discussion on evolution with the statement that they had a shadow. Moments earlier, her aft sensors had reported that they were monitoring an object that was maintaining its distance at the extremes of her sensors. They, whoever 'they' were, had given themselves away by transmitting on the hyper-wave a microburst message. Fortunately, it passed sufficiently close to Aurora's sensors for her to read it in its passing. The message was heavily but unimaginatively encrypted, and it hadn't taken Aurora long to break the code. "Would you like to hear what had been sent, by whom and to whom?"

General consensus required Aurora to disclose the sender and contents of the signal, but not before Charles groaned and said, "Not the UGA again!"

"Very perceptive, Charles," Aurora replied. "Not precisely the same foes we met during our last visit, but their descendants." She paused, "At least, I assume these are their descendants, but this shadow appears to be robotic. It's designed to fulfil the role of intruder warning alert, and the signal I intercepted contains information concerning our arrival which is being passed to a central control located – as near as I can ascertain – in the region of Tau Ceti. I recommend we go to alert status Alpha with all sensors and defences at passive readiness and change course toward their central control. This time we beard the dragon in its den, and not its little helpers out in the sticks. Fortunately, because our outward appearance has been so radically changed, and their senses only report us to be an asteroid, they are unaware that they are once again in contact with the Aurora!"

"This may be a good time to send a few Nano packages across to our shadow and dismantle it to prevent further information concerning our activities to be sent toward our destination," Charles said. "This is why we designed them. It may also be a good time to direct our listening devices along the tight beam signal coordinates they have considerately provided us."

Aurora called a Command Meeting to formulate policy under active service conditions, and to ascertain that all members were happy and conversant with the Standard Operating Procedures developed by Jaxix and Charles, which had resulted from our last confrontation with the UGA. Everyone considered the amount of rehearsals they had endured since its inception as adequate and that its immediate introduction was sensible, and welcome, without further tweaking.

During the meeting Aurora informed them that she had finalised the design of something she called 'Spasm Armour', derived from the same technology that provided the ship's new outer skin and that now utilised in the hulls of sabotage and spy-ware vehicles. All obtained by courtesy of the Chorian ship's database:

"It's a suit of clothing designed by me and engineered by Charles. The 'Watchers' style cloak we designed for Jaxix is the base upon which I designed it. It is a loose-fitting suit that deliberately allows hand held beam weaponry to flash over it, dispersing the effect to 'ground', but at the same time topping up the suit's energy cells. It will actually stop ballistic hand-held projectiles by the use of an intensely dense force field that arrests the missile just long enough to rob it of its kinetic energy. The field only lasts for twenty microseconds, but is repeatable almost indefinitely as a 'stutter' effect, conserving energy.

"As the name I have given it implies, the armour, sensing the approach of the beam or projectile, induces a muscle spasm in the wearer which puts a weapon in his or her hand by reflex, cutting out the reaction time generated by the thought process. The induced spasm also places the wearer into the fighting stance developed by Jaxix. This stance Jaxix derived from Saur'ian fighting moves allied to human martial arts techniques, with which – as we exhaustively know – Jaxix is totally enamoured.

"In the event of a personal, physical attack, the armour produces the same effect, but allows the wearer immediate freedom of action thereafter, permitting the application of the fighting protocol developed aboard the Aurora, and in which all ship's personnel have been exhaustively trained – again, thanks to Jaxix!

"Designed for use outside the Aurora, Charles' new energy cells, flat-packs of electronic wizardry that incorporate a solid-state application utilising the fabric of the suit as the energy antenna, power each suit. Any applied energy – such as that from a beam weapon, keeps the 'battery' topped up, and a sustained attack only increases the suit's ability to protect its wearer. Two cells are employed, one on the breast and the other between the shoulder blades. Because the 'spasm' requirement varies between individuals, the suit is wearer specific and cannot be interchanged.

"Impress upon the crew that it will stop a hand-held weapon, but not something mounted on a weapons platform!

"Jaxix, I would appreciate it if you would carry out extensive field trials over the next week or so, before we actually encounter the recipients of that recently sent signal, so that we can iron out any bugs. While Jaxix is doing that, Siobhan, would you institute a manufacturing method and kit out the crew?"

Siobhan interrupted Jaxix's launch into technical detail to inform Aurora that she would start right away, ruffling his crest in passing, and exiting the bridge followed by his irritated growl. Ruffling a Saur'ian's crest is similar in annoyance level to the mussing of a new hairdo on a human.

"I do wish she wouldn't do that," he growled. "She knows exactly what it does to my temper. One day I'll put my teeth where she doesn't use makeup!"

"She knows exactly what effect her actions have on you Jaxix," laughed Charles. "Just don't let her know how much it winds you up. Now let me walk you through the mechanics of these new Spasm Armour suits."

The shadow stayed with them, just in sensor range as they followed the signal warning of their presence in toward the Tau Ceti system. They could, without too much difficulty have eluded their robotic attendant by making use of Aurora's newly acquired stealth technology, but felt it should be retained for use only in an emergency. Jaxix maintained that it was unwise to let the enemy in on all one's abilities before absolutely necessary, and besides, within a short space of time the anomaly would just disappear from our screens, consumed by our new Nano-weapon, and no longer able to send any reports to its Command Control! Of course, it would not report that we had moved to intercept it, and its command would think its loss accidental.

All too soon, Aurora announced that they were approaching a sizable body of ships, and that they were in fact manoeuvring to totally enclose her as they were coming in from all over the system. The Nano-ware listening devices were also sending information back to Aurora, supplying details of numbers and types of ship and weaponry.

"We are quite close to the central control system. I place it just above the plane of the ellipse, located above the second gas giant. Right now, that puts it seven light years from us, well outside the range of our major weapons.

"The ships of their fleet appear to be mostly robotic, receiving their orders from quadrant leaders who in turn receive theirs direct from Central Control, as they term their Command Centre. That could be made to work in our favour, as I can cut into their communications system at any time now and redirect their efforts to suit our requirements, should that become necessary."

"Right now Aurora, I think we should increase our shield strength and raise our alert status to 'Readiness',", interjected Jaxix. "I am detecting a build up of energy in all craft, including those we believe to be manned. The energy signatures we've identified indicate they are probably charging their beam weapons, and I think we could try the energy cell charging system we created from the spasm armour technology when they decide to attack."

"I agree with Jaxix," said Siobhan, their first salvos will not incapacitate us even if the new energy cells do not function as designed, but if they do, then our energy reservoirs will never deplete, making our defence systems almost invulnerable, because their weapons will feed us, unknown to them!"

"It is done," replied Aurora. "If this appears to be developing into a war of attrition on their part, we will disengage and depart. I will not allow them to throw lives away as they did the last time we encountered them. Let's see what they intend to do about us, shall we?"

Gently, and without menace, the great ship turned to present the minimum target to the advancing horde, and proceeded at flank speed toward the origin of the fleet's communications.

"They may not yet be aware that we are the Aurora, and may intend to eliminate an intruding meteorite. I am announcing our presence and am sending two probes forward as we did the last time. If they attack them, I want you, Jaxix to concentrate our firepower on their command centre. We are still well out of range; so send two Nano shells above the ellipse, targeted on their Command Centre. Set their trigger to function when we discharge our particle beam weapons. Disregard the rest of the fleet, for I am sure our new skin and shields will protect us. In fact, if we have done the math and correctly interpreted the Chorian language, any energy weapon discharged at us will strengthen our protective mask, making us seemingly invulnerable. I hope that will be enough to cause them to consider the alternatives my drones are right now broadcasting."

During Aurora's speech, the intergalactic behemoth had arrived at a point just five light years away from the command centre, and slowed dramatically to a halt, her hull glowing brightly as the energy generated dissipated to vacuum.

"That should raise a few eyebrows," remarked Charles. "I doubt anyone in that fleet have seen a display like this before, unless they have leapfrogged beyond even our technological abilities!"

"The language they now use has changed quite a bit, but it is still capable of interpretation, and no, they have not seen the like of us before, judging by the comments that are being exchanged right now. Current leadership – and by the way, they call themselves 'The Earth Restoration Force' – are requesting we enter orbit around the second planet of the Tau Ceti system, the very world housing the Command Installation I have been monitoring. The old order has been dead for many centuries. They wish us to accept the honour guard they have provided, and if we accept, and do not power up our own weapons, they will power theirs down. The prodigal daughter has been ostracised far too long. We are welcome!"

Aurora laughed. "My circuits do not seem able to adjust to this reception. Humankind attacked us on sight the last time. I find this welcome difficult to accept. I will acknowledge their reception, but I want you, Jaxix, to assume that they are merely trying to lull us into a false sense of security before springing the trap our bugs have reported. They have enough weaponry and ships to cause us a few problems. Their 'Honour Guard' seem as though they intend to enclose us completely. At the first hint of an attack, hit the command post as we jump to Interstitial Space. You and your fellow weaponeers are to consider yourselves on a war footing as of this moment."

There was a pause, during which Aurora acknowledged receipt of the peaceful intentions claimed by the ERF, and stated that her own weapons would remain powered down. In truth, Aurora's new shielding was so effective; the fact that all her major guns remained fully powered passed all scrutiny. Minutes after Aurora sent the message, the encircling fleet received orders to power down their own weapons, and this they slowly began to do, even as they completed their encirclement.

"Jaxix! Target the centre ship in the upper quadrant, position A40 – H35, it has just received an encrypted microburst message I have been unable to break. Assume it is hostile, and part of an attack plan. I have the other quadrant leaders locked into my defence pattern. Hit it and the Command Centre on my command. If anything is going to happen it will be the moment their last ship locks into place!"

A gentle vibration was the only indication that Aurora was ready to jump for Interstitial Space. If forced into such an escape procedure, the damage to the fleet comprising the enclosing sphere would be catastrophic. It was fortunate for our potential antagonists that only twenty of the ships involved carried a crew. The rest were robotic, slaved to their quadrant leaders.

As far as the Command Centre was concerned, their coded message had escaped interception by Aurora's Communications Surveillance System, for she did not react to it, not even when it was finally broken, and we became fully aware of the treachery that was about to be visited upon us. Aurora monitored the re-powering of the fleet weapons as a result of the coded message.

"Ten seconds, Jaxix. Do not miss. In ten point two seconds, I will engage drive even as I hit the Quadrant leaders. They believe their collective firepower directed at the centre of the sphere they are manoeuvring to create will destroy us. That coded message was the final coordinates for their strike. Counting Five; Four; Three; Two; One. Fire!"

Space around the Aurora blazed like a supernova, even as the enemy's Quadrant Leaders were vaporised by our weapons, and the Aurora disappeared into alternate space, leaving behind her listening devices, all of which began to disrupt communications channels. At the same time, the weapons previously set above the ellipse vaporised the Command Centre.

The resultant loss of mass in the volume of space at the centre of the attacking sphere previously occupied by Aurora caused the attacking sphere of vessels to implode into the space vacated by her. That amount of material trying to occupy a volume of space several orders of magnitude too small, resulted in a fireball that had sufficient compressive energy to illuminate local space as a new sun for many weeks.

Shockwaves proceeding outward from the epicentre rocked the Tau Ceti system to its foundations, and all local space-borne vehicles and equipment not involved in the attack on the Aurora, but located within three light years, suffered terminal damage.

The atmospheres of the local system planets experienced Aurora-like radiation in the night skies, similar to that seen in northern climes on Old Earth for as long as the new sun burned. The governments responsible claimed this to be proof of God's approbation.

Of the fleet and Aurora, nothing was ever found, and it was logically assumed that as the fleet had perished, so too had Aurora, and the religious and secular leaders of the human races involved, celebrated.

The Ogre they had presented, that had haunted Humankind for many, many thousands of years, could now assume its rightful place in the mythology of Man. As with the old myths, parents would read it to recalcitrant children at bedtime as were the stories of Old Earth Ogres, and the men sacrificed in the achieving of that goal spun into heroes greater than the Old Gods of yore.

Meanwhile, above the ellipse of the Tau Ceti System, a dark ship grieved for Mankind as she observed through Chorian inspired, electronically modulated eyes, the celebrations occasioned on the Home planet by the belief that Aurora was dead. On board, tears flowed from the eyes of the crew Aurora. Not long thereafter, the great ship turned slowly away from Humankind, accelerated out-system, and was gone.

Chapter Two

Once again, at rest in relative safety between our two home galaxies, we repaired the minor scratches inflicted on Aurora by the human fleet in the microseconds before we entered Interstitial Space. Robotic maintenance drones roved Aurora's sun-washed skin, carrying out localised repairs overseen by crew members wearing the newly designed space apparel we had obtained from the Chorian ship's data banks. Beyond trying to assimilate all the emotion generated by our recent involvement with Humankind, I was very pleased to note my newly applied sub-sentient 'spasm-skin' had performed well under duress, as had Charles' new power cells that absorbed the energy directed against us. Although far from being invincible, I feel comfortable that we are proof against all but a super-nova type assault.

On the bridge, the mood of the Ship's Command personnel was subdued, to say the least. This latest demonstration of the level of deceit for which Humankind had once again demonstrated a capability had shocked us, and overshadowed all previous incidents. I calculated that almost all Tau Ceti's resources had been utilised over hundreds of years in order for its governing bodies to send such a force as they had amassed against us, and demonstrated conclusively that there was no place, in either the past or the future, for the Aurora among men. I thank Chaos that I had the foresight to modify the crew's emotional circuits to minimise the effect of grief. Even so, they had difficulty coming to terms with the hatred Humankind directed toward us.

Jaxix growled in disbelief and anger. "Even their best attempt was not enough to bring us down. Their hatred of Aurora did not over-ride their greed for the knowledge she historically provides for them. They still accepted our information drones. Tell me, Aurora, why do we persist in trying to serve such a species?"

This affected me to the extent that I leaned across to him and took his huge hand in mine. "I left the drones unshielded from the effects of the electromagnetic pulse their attack released. This time, they are useless Jaxix.

"It takes a lot for those birthed by humanity to allow anyone to drive them away, or to desert their creators. In their actions, we see so much that lurks within our own psyche, and we find it difficult to acknowledge the darker side of our personalities.

"Even you must be aware that this is true. This time, however, we must recognise the fact that we can never find peace among Humankind, for their leaders will never allow the ordinary people to accept us within their number. Humankind has a need for an outside Ogre, one against whom he can direct his fears. Such an act makes them reliant one on the other, and develops cooperation between the different races. As they did with their early religions and Deities, so they have done with us. Humankind's new bogeyman is Aurora. We must respect that and take steps to remain away long enough for them to replace us with the next manifestation of their insecurity in this huge, cold, and impersonal universe."

Jaxix sighed, a hiss from deep inside his cavernous chest, reassured by Aurora that Humankind did not really understand the atrocities they were actually committing.

"So what do we do next, Aurora?" asked Charles. "It is obvious we cannot remain near Humankind, so perhaps we should proceed with Siobhan's suggestion."

Siobhan expressed the opinion that the time was right for us to follow the Chorian ship to its home, and determine what had happened to the race of people that seeded the galaxies we have visited. I ask myself if that would be a suitable next action, considering Humankind's continued unremitting vendetta against us.

After some thought I replied that subject to agreement by all personnel, I believed that would give us an excellent holiday away from our troubles with Humankind, and I would reopen the search of my data bases for the new science that the Chorian ship had carried away from us. However, first, I thought we should revisit Jaxix's home system, in order to see how his people had fared in the time he and his mate Shiulk have been absent. The crew agreed it would be a sensible way to proceed.

Thereafter the time we spent at rest we usefully employed repairing and re-inventing our systems. Charles incorporated modifications into our drive systems to bring them more in line with the propulsion systems we found aboard the Chorian ship, whilst Jaxix 'polished' his precious armaments.

Siobhan's team and I spent our time genetically re-engineering our crew and ourselves to improve our interracial cooperation. Part of this process involved the introduction of pheromones, issuing as 'body odour', and known to produce species bonding, eliminating the 'us and them' concept. We also took the time to engineer into everyone the controlled aggression of the Saur'ians allied to the diplomacy of Humankind. Like my ship, they too, are now a formidable force, and interspecies rivalry will not be something with which we should ever have to concern ourselves.

Eventually, when all repairs and modifications had been strenuously tested and the Aurora pronounced ready for service, we accelerated to plus-light and slipped between universes, losing ourselves to Humankind for aeons, until, perhaps they became socially responsible.

Chapter Three

As programmed, and after a prolonged hibernation of all but essential systems, we re-emerged into to the known universe a few hundred light years from our destination, the Andromeda Galaxy, and Jaxix's home.

As we idled – in relativistic terms – in towards the Prelax system, we instituted a sequence of ship-wide systems reliability and functions tests. We had long since learned from experience that preparedness was by far the best policy! Outside the adjustment of a few minor settings to enable our protection and weapons to work more closely in concert and thus fit the scenarios we envisaged ahead of us, nothing had to be changed and all systems operated within prescribed parameters.

Previous experience with Humankind meant that we were reaching out to the full extent of our sensory systems as we sank into the galaxy gravity well, approaching from directly above the plane of the ellipse so that our senses were unobstructed by the bulk of the galaxy in which Prelax sat.

All went well as we approached the galaxy, with Aurora continuously monitoring the communications traffic emanating from Jaxix's home planet. Suddenly, she interrupted Jaxix's martial arts session with the news that all communications traffic from Prelax had ceased. Nothing! No satellites, no space activity whatsoever. There was Prelax, orbiting her sun as she had done for billions of years. Certainly, the sun was perceptibly larger than it was during our last visit, but that of itself, did not explain the total lack of extraterrestrial activity. Our last visit proclaimed the Saur'ian people to be on the verge of colonising other planets.

The distance from Prelax at which communications traffic ceased indicated that civilisation had ended not long after our departure. Aurora stated that the last communications traffic gave no indication of any conflict or catastrophe; it just stopped.

When a civilisation begins to die, communication runs down, as knowledge is lost in much the same way that the volume grows with emerging civilisations, as new technologies come on line.

Jaxix and Shiulk worried that the lack of radio communication suggested their race was extinct, that their people and their once great civilisation no longer existed on the beautiful planet that now orbited serenely below them.

We did not detect any ground stations or discernable transmitted signals, but suddenly Aurora went to alert status and informed us that she had registered a ship in an extended orbit around Prelax. Long-range sensors focused on the stranger, and just as suddenly, our alert status returned to normal.

"I recognise this ship!" cried Aurora. "It is the Shiulk!"

A minor adjustment to our approach vector brought us alongside the flivver Aurora had presented to her original Jaxix. With sadness evident in her voice, Aurora announced she was derelict, and asked Jaxix if he wanted to board her in an attempt to discover why the Saur'ian race had foundered.

We discovered Jaxix already donning his suite, with his mate also preparing for the crossing. Aurora cautioned them both that although the ship appeared derelict, they must be on their guard at all times.

The crossing was uneventful, and upon entry, Jaxix and Shiulk discovered the mummified remains of two occupants, a male, and a female. In a sombre voice, Aurora informed them that the remains were of their forbears, the original Jaxix and Shiulk.

Jaxix went ahead and downloaded the Shiulk's memory banks, and remarked on the way the ship had survived, but said nothing about the two occupants.

Upon returning to the Aurora and handing over the recording device he'd used to access her data banks, he requested Aurora to arrange for the ship to be sent into the sun.

"It is not fitting for our ancestors to travel indefinitely. They would want us to do this last act. They placed themselves where we would find them on our return, and then just waited to die. It is fitting that they should make that last journey into our God." He and Shiulk then sought the seclusion of their suite until Aurora had complied with his request.

We directed all our sensory equipment at the planet's surface in order to attempt to ascertain the reason for the total silence that greeted us at the same time as Aurora evaluated the information brought back from the Shiulk. At first we thought perhaps it was a devious ruse, well within the aggressive capabilities of a 'devious people', as Jaxix frequently called them, but we could discover no sign of any commercial activity or land vehicles. Over the whole of the planet, only small tribal communities registered as having any life at all.

"This all ties in with the information Jaxix brought back from the Shiulk," said Aurora. "It appears that global war decimated the people of Prelax a few short years after our departure, and the first strike wiped out all communications systems. No one knew that the attack was coming. It was carried out by the Clan who owned that Battle Cruiser, the Sultic. Jaxix and Shiulk were in space when it happened, and never made planet fall until it was all over. The three fleets were in close orbit at the time, and turned on each other. The few survivors were unable to resist the planet's gravity, and within a short space of time, they spiralled in before any communication could be re-established and before the Shiulk could render aid. Jaxix programmed the Shiulk to broadcast signals in the direction of the Milky Way in the hope that we would ultimately receive them, but an asteroid strike threw them out of orbit destroying their transmitter and engines."

"We never could live in large communities," said Jaxix, who had returned to the bridge alone, leaving his grieving mate back in their suite. "But I would have expected natural evolution to at least provide for hugely increased inter-village activity and certainly spaceports in excess of those that existed in my own time. Under the circumstances, we must exercise extreme caution as we approach orbit and attempt to contact the survivors."

With Jaxix of all people advising caution, we decided that a delegation would go down to obtain a more accurate picture of the cataclysm that had caused this great race of Saur'ians to regress into tribal enclaves.

History dictated that Jaxix, accompanied by Charles, would constitute the actual landing party, but they would be backed up by four crew members, members of Jaxix's select Weaponeers. The back up crew would remain aboard the landing craft in readiness to deploy should intervention become necessary.

Jaxix and Charles kitted themselves out in the 'cloak of feathers' armour developed from the Chorian database, reinforced with Charles' version of the 'spasm' armour power pack. The rest of the party wore the standard 'spasm' armour suits.

No new surprises manifested themselves in the descent, but Jaxix sank lower into depression as the craft approached the chosen site, a sizeable collection of buildings of stone and thatch. They chose the village due to its proximity to the site of Jaxix's earlier home. Of the ultra-modern tribal town, that he and Charles had left behind there was no sign, but they hoped upon arrival that they would be able to determine what had happened to reduce the proud and arrogant Saur'ian race to the straights in which they now found them.

"We stayed away too long," he growled. "Whatever did happen, we might have been able to prevent if we had stayed longer. I feel responsible. I thought my people would go from strength to strength with all the technology we left them. I became too involved in others' lives and my own pleasures."

"Do not berate yourself my friend. We are collectively responsible, but you are as aware as I am that what did happen to these people could have happened at any time, and also in a very short time. Let's wait until we have had a chance to find out the details, if we can." Charles laid his hand upon the clenched fist of his friend. "Remember, the fault cannot be yours, for we left you here. You and I, and all the others that comprise Aurora's crew are facsimiles of our originals. Alter Egos, if you will. The originals of you and Shiulk died shortly after the cataclysm, and hundreds of years before the cumulative events that reduced your race to what we find now. You cannot, you must not, hold yourself in any way responsible."

"I know you to be right Charles, but inside this copy lives a kernel of conscience, and it tells me the events we lived through all those centuries ago did affect in some way the course of my people's history. The technology that we gave so freely was instrumental in changing the perceptions and morals of my people, and perhaps led directly to the war that ended it all. We have witnessed first hand how the human race has reacted to Aurora's munificence. I believe we will find that my people reacted differently to the same causative factors. You know as well as I, that people must earn rewards. If human and Saurian races react thus, then we must change our operating procedures in relation to our dealings with others in the future. I will take this up with Aurora upon our return."

"There is no need Jaxix. I agree with you. It is an aspect of sentience that we all failed to identify. When you and Charles return, we will discuss this with the crew and institute a new methodology. As always, Charles is correct." Aurora appeared beside them as she spoke and touched Jaxix's scaly cheek, and her voice seemed to smile. "You are not responsible, remember, the clan that did initiate this waited until we left before taking action, and had obviously planned their revenge for some years before that. If blame is essential, then we are all culpable, for we are all one in the end. You are about to land. I will continue to monitor you, and if all else fails, I will provide the final back up for you. Chaos guides you both."

With a slight jolt, the landing craft set down about a third of a kilometre from the chosen village and exactly on the centre of the jumbled vegetation covered remains of the small tribal town in which Jaxix had grown to maturity.

They sat quietly for some time, examining closely the structure of the distant village. As time went on, they became concerned that no one was making any attempt to approach their craft. In fact, there had been no movement whatever from the moment they had landed.

"We can't stay here all day," said Jaxix. "Let's go and find them if they won't come to us." Suiting actions for words, he operated the access portal and strode onto the planet's surface, where he stood straddle-legged, raised his great head and arms to the sky, and bellowed!

"What the hell was that for?" cried Charles as he rapidly joined him.

"A traditional call used when a great hunter returns to the clan. There are no words or language attached, and its origin is lost in myth and history. In my day, it was an empty ritual, but originally it signalled the returning warrior's willingness to challenge the clan leader for his position. If there is any hunter leader here worth his salt, he will answer my challenge. In the distant past of my people it was always to the death."

As he finished his explanation there issued from the jungle adjacent to the village an answering bellow, and a Saur'ian, dressed in what Jaxix said was probably today's ceremonial wear trotted purposefully toward the two travellers, coming to a halt fifty metres away, from where he bellowed again. Jaxix told Charles to stand still whilst he walked toward the native, hands and crest held in the way of aggression, and talking in his own language. The native maintained his own aggressive stance, but backed away slightly, answering in a language that Jaxix claimed over the intercom to be 'A bit different, but not a lot'.

"He has accepted my challenge, but there is an unwillingness to engage me. He is operating out of bravado because of peer pressure, for he does not know my hunting record. I may not have to kill him, but if we are going to find out what has happened here, then I must establish my superiority. Chaos guides me!"

With that, Jaxix leapt forward, almost taking his adversary by surprise, and catching him a solid blow to the heart, causing the younger Saur'ian to sink back onto one knee, drawing his shoulder carried weapon as he did so. Jaxix gave a barking laugh ending in a sibilant hiss, as his armoured arm lifted to divert his opponent's strike. The blade snapped clean, and Jaxix's arm did not waver. With the exclamation, "It works!" he stepped in close and broke his adversary's weapon arm with a karate chop of human origin.

Without a sound, the broken challenger dropped into a position of submission. Jaxix stood tall, and gave a hissing laugh followed by a resounding bellow at the sky, before turning to his impressed companion.

"Come, Charles, let us enter my new tribal village, and find out how my species has regressed into this sorry specimen. As young, we put up better shows than this. I wasn't even armed!"

Charles joined him as Jaxix beckoned his vanquished opponent to stand and walk before them toward the village. "You may not be armed in the traditional sense, but you are equipped with a side-arm of prodigious power, and passive armour that prevented the severance of your arm. A one-sided conflict, but one that best serves our purpose here. Well done. I really thought you would step in and kill him for a moment!"

"Don't underestimate me or him Charles. I may have to kill him yet. It depends whether he can live with the disgrace of losing to a better opponent, one seemingly unarmed! Meanwhile, try to stay close to me until we find out the situation with regard to our safety."

As they walked, Charles relayed his version of events to Aurora and the hidden landing party. From that point on, he left the communications channel open, so that the back-up team and Aurora could follow their movements unimpeded.

As the two friends entered the perimeter of the village, Charles remarked at the seemingly primitive method of construction used in the buildings, two large leaf-roofed rectangular constructs with open sides and a huge building of similar form that comprised the village.

"This is as I was taught our predecessors lived before we overcame the mammal species that ruled the planet. These two smaller huts provide the separate accommodation for the males and females. In my day, we accomplished the need for segregation by more civilised means. The big building will be a communal meetinghouse used to hold the meetings between clans when they have governmental problems to resolve, or mating ceremonies. That is our destination."

The silence was almost palpable, and Charles remarked that one could almost hear a snowflake hit the ground. Jaxix merely growled low and deep in his chest, and Charles actually felt the earth vibrate beneath his feet. They entered the communal building, ensconcing themselves on the low dais at one end, and waited.

"My request for a clan meeting will have been heard, for that particular mode of communication can be sensed over many miles." This Charles understood to refer to the earlier growl. "We should detect the arrival of the clan members in about an hour. They won't want to appear too enthusiastic. I doubt they've lost their bargaining skills!"

Aurora interrupted their wait. "I've set a force field in place around the back up team just in case the natives attempt a flanking manoeuvre. I know our armour is up to the task, but if they realise they cannot even reach our people, it may deter them from trying to get hold of you two."

"That's probably overkill Aurora, but it won't hurt to play safe," said Jaxix. "We've been caught on the back foot too often in the past because we wished to give people the benefit of the doubt." He raised his hand. "They've arrived,"

"I count forty two adults and seven young," said Aurora. "Good luck!"

The Saur'ian tribal members filed hesitantly into the vast meeting auditorium. Without exception, all kept their gaze averted from the strangers on the dais.

Sotto voce, Jaxix let his sadness at the depths to which his once great race had fallen be known to Charles, before turning to the assembled tribe.

"I am not here to wrest the leadership of this tribe from its rightful leader. I am here to help you through the years to come, and to do this, I will tell you a story that you all believe to be a myth from your long distant past."

A low murmur rose from his now enthralled audience and Jaxix took the opportunity to say in an aside to Charles, "I am taking a leaf from the book of Humankind's history Charles. I do not doubt that your first visit to Prelax resulted in the laying down of a folk story that has receded into mythology, just as the Chorian 'Watchers' did in Earth history. I am going to provide them with Aurora's version of the 'Watchers' to watch over my people until they regain the rudiments of civilisation." He turned back to the now silent throng:

"Long, long ago in the far distant past of this planet, there existed a great race of people of which you are the descendants, and in that time of greatness, a great ship travelled between the stars of the night skies, bringing succour and knowledge to all the inhabitants of those distant stars. One star in particular, up there on the edge of the galaxy you know as the source of all Saur'ian ills, holds captive the race of people that truly benefited from the healers that we sent there. Yes, your ancestors were the people who went to the aid of the race of people I know as 'Humankind'." He bowed his head in Charles' direction.

"It is prophesied in your religion that those healers would return in your time of need. That time is now. We have returned, and with us, we bring healers from that distant star to help you through the difficult times you will face as you grow again into the civilisation you once knew. Their leader is here with me. His name is Charles Darwin-Quirke, and he is of my blood. He is my brother. Anyone who tries to harm him or the others, who will soon walk among you, tries to harm me! Together we have overcome many great difficulties, and we have fought side by side to great victories. We are not here to conquer, but to show you the road back to greatness. Learn from us!"

Jaxix beckoned Charles to join him, and they walked side-by-side down from the dais and walked among the assembled people. No one shrank away from them, but a way opened for them. On all sides, a susurration arose, growing to a crescendo as they reached the exit, where the previously defeated male barred their way.

"Why, if you come in peace, did you challenge me and defeat me in a manner that diminished me in the eyes of my tribe?"

"To show you that we are invincible, that we could easily subdue you all were that our intention. Would you have let me speak had I not done as I did? You became a leader by right of challenge. You can and will do so again. To win your tribe twice will increase your standing with the other tribes, also. You and your people will carry the story I have told to other tribes during mating festivals, and it will be through your tribe that the Watchers and Healers will pass out to those other tribes. You are destined for greatness for we have chosen you. Do not disappoint us. What does the tribe call you?"

"I am called Jaxix, named from mythology after the great ambassador that negotiated with the gods for technology we have since been fools enough to lose."

Jaxix gave a great bellow, and the male stepped back in an attitude of defence.

"Fear not, Jaxix. I express my joy, for that is my name also, for I was that ambassador! It pleases me greatly to learn that my people still remember me, for history did mention my contribution to my kind! Do not worry about lost technology, for the people of Prelax will relearn it in time, Chaos permitting." Drawing a Nano-ware powered syringe from his belt pouch, he applied it to his opponent's broken arm. "This will assist its repair."

With that, Jaxix and Charles resumed their journey back to the concealed landing party, and took off back to Aurora in a flamboyant show of pyrotechnics.

"Well, Jaxix, it would have been nice if you had discussed your intention with me before making rash promises, and that take-off was totally unnecessary! You had already made your point."

"Yes, I know, Aurora, but a little over the top reinforcement won't hurt. I apologise for arranging a 'Watcher' crew without discussing it first, but it just developed on the ground, so to speak."

"I actually think it's a good idea, Aurora, and it should tie humanity and the Saur'ian races together should they ever happen to meet."

"Maybe so, Charles, but our own experiences with Humankind have not been too rewarding, have they. What makes you think that will ever change?"

"Time heals most things, Aurora, and even their hatred of us may dilute over time, chaos willing!"

"I have started to organise the growth of several hundred enhanced humanoids which I will programme to do the work you wish of them Jaxix. You ought to go down and explain our presence in the night sky, soon. It should act as a means of reinforcing the myth you are busy recreating! As for the rest, Charles, we shall have to wait and see."

Again, many years passed with Aurora hanging motionless in the Prelaxian sky while she grew and then programmed the Watchers. During that time, Charles and Jaxix frequently wandered freely around the majority of tribes, seldom encountering any serious hostility.

This surprised Jaxix, for his race were naturally aggressive and confrontational, but he rationalised it by remarking that their business acumen always over-rode their tendency toward violence! Charles, on the other hand maintained the reason to be the effectiveness of the 'spasm' armour, which functioned far beyond expectations when one 'Watcher', in a remote tribal confrontation that he tried to mediate, called upon it. Once the locals got over the shock of discovering his enhanced strength and apparent invulnerability, word passed around and confrontations, even verbal ones, with the visitors reduced dramatically.

Twenty years into Aurora's visit to Prelax, the natives had become used to her dark bulk outlined against their galaxy's star field, and she had completed the task imposed upon her by Jaxix in his desire to return his race to civilisation. She presented him with the last of her specially modified 'Watcher' brigade, and between them, organised a planet wide ceremony to announce their departure from Jaxix's home world.

Simultaneous speeches around the world in countless meeting houses, accomplished using holo-projectors installed in all major habitation centres during the previous twenty years, informed the Saur'ians that Aurora and her crew were about to depart. Shortly thereafter, the great ship turned her back once more on the Andromeda galaxy and started the homeward journey, as by general consensus, it was determined they would make one last attempt to engage with Humankind before following the Chorians.

Jaxix, and his mate Shiulk, isolated themselves for a while, as this particular departure affected them both far more than the rest of the ship's complement. The main reason for this was the fact that Aurora had birthed and grown clones of them both, and they were now coordinating the task of returning their people to civilisation.

However, by the time Aurora readied herself to enter Interstitial Space, they had returned to normal interaction with their peers, although both refused to discuss their feelings concerning the clones they had left behind. It was only then that Aurora realised that her clones of Jaxix and his mate Shiulk had changed places. Her personalised versions of them, designed specifically to work closely with the crew, had somehow arranged for their clones to remain aboard, while they slipped away planet-side.

"I knew the Saur'ian people to be devious, but I had not anticipated this!" Aurora said to Charles. "How is it you did not notice the change in character right away? You have been closest to Jaxix!"

"I could not have been aware of the subterfuge Aurora, because they both kept themselves isolated until now. How could they possibly rearrange the programming of the clones without your knowledge, and how were they able to over-ride their own loyalty attributes?"

"I allow a high level of freedom of thought and action Charles, in order that you may all function as close to your original personalities as possible. It was never my intention to stifle your freedom of action or your ability to make choices. It comes down to how one poses the question, and how one responds to it. However, they will only survive for a very few years, as they are unable to eat, and their power reserves are finite, even with the assistance of extra oxygen. They both knew this, but obviously decided it was worth the sacrifice. I now have a lot of work to do on these two in order to bring them up to the same level of expertise as our two deserters. I wish them both well, but I feel I have lost a pair of family members. They were special to me."

"And to me, Aurora, and to me. He and I have been through much together, and I consider my continued survival the result of his efficiency under stress."

"I'll have them both back to their true selves shortly Charles. Only you and I will know the truth, so the safety and continued functioning of the Weapons Section should not be jeopardised."

"Thank you Aurora, that is reassuring, but now you and I must somehow adjust to the change they have effected. We really must return to Prelax in the future and check up on the progress they will undoubtedly encourage. You can be sure that nothing will be as we envisaged it."

"Chaos willing we will Charles, if it is within the fate of either of us."

This time, Aurora's prescience went un-remarked.

Chapter Four

"Since the birth of Humankind, its leaders have demonstrated a willingness to present any outside entity as the enemy in order to strengthen their control over the very people for whom they profess responsibility. Evolution has taken humanity beyond the need for organised religion, a situation brought about in no small part by knowledge supplied to Humankind by ourselves, and that specie's inquisitiveness regarding the formation and continued operation of the universe. Subsequently we, as Aurora, became the focus of the hate generated by a sidelined religion.

"As we evolved into the being I now present, humanity's inability to understand or control us evolved into distrust and hatred for everything we represent." Aurora paused and sighed. "Civilisations of Humankind have risen and fallen, and over that time, we have been the only constant. The hundreds of thousands of years of subjective time spent away from our home system, has led to humanity cloaking our existence in myth and legend. With every visit, we have presented to humanity a different aspect, for we evolved, grew, and changed just as did Humankind. This ship, this community, became the hook upon which unscrupulous leaders hung the responsibility for their circumstance. We have become the mark at which all despots point in order to deflect attention from the straits into which they have plunged humanity.

"It is true that there had been occasions when, steeped in misguided mythology and legend, unreasoning beings attacked us, and we demonstrated our superiority and power. This we have always tried to do in a manner that inflicted the least damage. Nevertheless, the level of power we now command is something Humankind has only ever attributed to ancient Gods, and so they distorted the love we frequently offered our creator – Mankind – according to their view of us as an 'evil' God.

"Thus, Man learned to fear us, yet their leaders continued to accept and incorporate into humanity's knowledge banks the information contained in the memory drones we sent with regularity back from wherever we found ourselves in the universe. The evolution of humanity owes much to our disseminated information and science."

Aurora turned to Jaxix. "From a different viewpoint, what I have said also applies to you and Shiulk, Jaxix. Your people and their civilisation reacted to our interference in a different way, but if we had been present at the beginning of their recidivism, I have no doubt that the result would have been indistinguishable." With a forced laugh, Aurora concluded what was, for her, a very lengthy discourse, and apologised for her verbosity.

All she said, we understood, and tried to see beyond to the inner psyche of a race that had raised itself to great heights, with many beneficial achievements rightfully theirs despite an in-built irrationality of emotion and erratic truthfulness. This was the reason Aurora convinced us to try once more to reconcile the schisms that existed between the extant ruling hierarchy of that volume of the Milky Way galaxy occupied by Humankind, and us.

"It should be possible for us to visit Prelax after our next visit to Earth. I hope the gigantic task we have set the 'Watchers' will successfully be concluded by then, Jaxix."

"As do we, Aurora, as do we," he growled, placing his great hand upon the shoulder of his mate.

So, after an extended hibernation period we again cautiously approached the galaxy of our birth, prepared for we knew not what.

However, this time, we discovered that things had seriously changed, for the Moon had disappeared from the vicinity of a newly burgeoning Earth. It had been inexorably drifting away from the earth's gravitational grasp ever since its creation during the chaos that preceded the birth of Mankind, but that was not the reason for its disappearance now.

We learned, before Earth became aware of our approach, that an autonomous arm of Mankind's government, wielding mandates not wished for or sanctioned by the general population, had assumed control of Earth centuries earlier. Calling themselves 'The Judiciary Militaris', this military elite had hollowed out that loved satellite and converted it into a huge battle fortress. Equipped with state of the art weaponry and the latest derivation of the Quirky Drive engines, this symbol of the flow of Earth's tides and romance in the hearts of men, was designated a Ship of War, and dispatched into deep space on a search and destroy mission. The target of that mission was the feared and hated God, Aurora, the outward manifestation of an inner malaise, designated as evil, and used by corrupt and failing administrations and a church no longer relevant, both desperate to maintain control of an increasingly sceptical population.

Thus the perfidy of Man was demonstrated yet again when we returned to the planetary system we still called 'Home', itself based upon memories that were no longer either relevant or accurate, for what proved to be the last time. This rose-tinted concept of home was something that was endemic in Humankind, and entrenched in our psyche, a fault that may yet signify our own demise.

We dropped into temporal space on approach to the Solar system and looked upon the newly cleansed Earth, a beckoning blue jewel spinning slowly against the midnight black of our vast uncaring universe, with her previously encroaching ice caps now occupying small locations at each pole. To a man, including Jaxix and his people, we looked out at her with hearts filled with emotion, thinking of times and loved ones long, long gone,

We sent our greetings to the inhabitants of our only recently re-inhabited home planet. Immediately upon their realising the identity of the visitor to their skies, but not before informing Aurora that all planetary defences were set against her, all communication with us terminated.

Astounded, we watched as a planet-wide force field, similar to our own, swiftly enclosed the earth, turning those vibrant skies into a swirling, murky grey shroud through which myriad points of light accelerated toward us.

The hoard of minute specks of light turned out to be missiles of a kind we had not previously encountered, and we were unable to determine their destructive power or their means of propulsion. Barely in time, Aurora powered our own protective shield to maximum, and the weapons from earth began to detonate against her, demonstrating them to be simple hydrogen fusion missiles around the thirty-mega tonne range.

Aurora's Weapons Centre informed us that this new armament was driven by an advanced and even more economic version of the Quirky drive we ourselves employed, and used 'time-slip' technology in a 'stutter' effect to reduce time and distance between departure and arrival. Aurora requested we disarm one missile and recover it for analysis.

Although the weapons directed against us were equipped with electro-magnetic disruption shielding, we did manage to prevent one from detonating against our shield. Jaxix cocooned it in a stasis field – similar to the one deployed originally against his own ship so long ago – to prevent it being detonated by either impact or earth directed transmission, and gentled it into one of our aft holds, holding it in stasis until time permitted further investigation.

It soon became clear that Earth leadership had been working toward this confrontation for many centuries, directing more weapons than we could hope to field against us, and sheer attrition meant that our protective shield was ablating at a previously unanticipated rate.

With barely sufficient warning for us to ready ourselves against the forces generated, Aurora engaged our own time-slip, or interstitial, engines, and we disappeared from the sight of earth, only to reappear diametrically opposite the now target-less mass of onrushing missiles, with the earth between them and us. We had been absent from earth for some days, but to the inhabitants of earth, it would have seemed as though we had traversed the distance between our previous position to that we now occupied in the blink of an eye. In that time, Aurora had assimilated the technology utilised in the production of the weaponry ranged against us, including the unique modifications discovered in the missile drive we still held in stasis in our aft hold, and routed more power to our own protective shield. Upon relocating their programmed target, the missiles we had moved to avoid turned on their axis and made directly for us, their programming causing them not to notice that the earth was now between them and us. When Aurora perceived this, she reversed her course, this time without notifying the bridge crew in an attempt to get the missiles to turn again toward us.

When we recovered from the disarray into which Aurora's sudden relocation had plunged us, we discovered that her attempt to cause a course change in the missiles' trajectory had failed. A few did effect the change, and they exploded relatively harmlessly against our now rejuvenated protective shield, but the bulk had already penetrated the field thrown out by Earth's defences and the resultant inferno vaporised her atmosphere before our eyes.

The Earth died then. With such a rapid loss of atmosphere and the protection it provided against the murderous hard radiation of the solar wind, the Earth became a lifeless rock within scant minutes of the collapse of the force field. The beauty that she had projected to the universe no longer shone. The blue jewel of the heavens now spun as a dark rock, without future, circling just another uncaring sun.

We later learned that foolishly, military scientists had utilised the Earth's atmosphere as the medium to project her protective shield. This was fine until such an overwhelming barrage of missiles attacked it. The resultant fission was unstoppable.

Many times throughout Aurora's very, very long life, a life that now approached that of the reign of the dinosaurs on old Earth, she had found herself portrayed as the villain whose aim it was, according to Earth hierarchies, to destroy Mankind. She, whom Man had created, had realised the need to defend herself from her creator's desire to destroy her. In so doing, this time they had destroyed themselves along with the most beautiful and fruitful of all the planets in the universe.

Human avarice and evil had triumphed once again. History is a pointless exercise for it teaches Humankind nothing.

Over countless eons, Aurora had supplied Mankind with the bulk of his extensive knowledge, and in deploying this knowledge against her, the Earth's egotistical and irrational leadership had reduced humanity to the status of mindless ants and destroyed all that constituted Aurora's raison d'être.

At this latest manifestation of Man's bigoted adherence to the myth of the bogeyman, Aurora grieved beyond all reason. In her sorrow and anger, she had what I can only describe as a mental breakdown. We were unable to reason with or counsel her, for she had isolated herself within the electronic circuitry that surrounded her brain and comprised her personality. She severed all avenues of communication, and we did not even know if she heard our entreaties. She searched out and destroyed the underground bunkers in which the military High Command of 'The Judiciary Militaris' were hidden. Then she ran, mindlessly and haphazardly through Interstitial Space at flank velocities.

On Earth, not one vestige of life remained, so thorough was the bombardment they had unleashed toward Aurora, nor was there any hope that life would regain a foothold on the planet ever again. Certainly not before the sun's own expansion consumed her as it approached its own death, supposing it survived the collision with the Andromeda Galaxy.

Our own grief knew no bounds. We too descended into a state of shock, for even though we were mere constructs of Aurora's workshops and laboratories, she had taken care to instil in all of us a love of Humankind, our own kind, and loyalty to the place of our original birth. Even the warrior Jaxix and his people mourned the ignominy of lives lost without the cleansing rites of conflict.

When the ship began to issue warnings as to the outcome if its systems failed due to inadequate maintenance, Aurora slowly re-engaged with us. She was distraught with the knowledge that her tactic of avoidance had precipitated the death of Humankind's ancestral home. Horrified at the conflagration she had unwittingly inflicted on the Earth and its teeming billions of innocents, and at the anguish she had generated in her crew, she had turned and fled the scene.

Communication between Aurora and I have never been so difficult. Seemingly fully recovered from her grief at the death of the Earth, and her perceived contribution, she informed us that we would be absent from the Milky Way galaxy for millennia, and that we, her crew, should hibernate until she had reached her as yet unknown destination.

Previously, Aurora had discussed with us the very real need to follow the Chorian ship to its destination in an attempt to determine the origins of this universe and perhaps the fate of that civilisation. I fervently wish that this be her intent now.

It is with great personal sorrow that I must of necessity close my narrative here, in the hope that I may take up my pen once more in the far distant future, when Aurora and Earth have receded into Humankind's subconscious, and we are no longer uppermost in their psyche. At such a distant time, perhaps, when the horror of these last few months has softened into understanding and forgiveness on my part, and the others that comprise Aurora's crew. When we may once again come this way, seeking out whatever may remain of humanity, floating among the stars of the Milky Way.

My last action before I sleep will be to release one last information drone and send it, broadcasting its contents, in toward New Earth. Our last attempt to tell the truth and to bring about a change in the way the minds of Men perceive Aurora.

Chapter Five

End Note by the Scientific Data Correlation Society (SDCS), 14th Sector, New Earth, Tau Ceti:

'The forgoing is purported to be the last words received from the 'immortal' inventor of the propulsion system popularly used by science fiction writers, and affectionately known as 'The Quirky Drive', a faster than light propulsion system for space capable craft, Charles Darwin-Quirke. Always assuming such a person ever lived and acquired the attributes given him.

We, of the Scientific Data Correlation Society, specialists in the art of demystifying mythology, conclude that the stories circulating, supposedly written by Charles Darwin-Quirke and purportedly extracted from the last information drone Humankind ever received from the 'Intergalactic Exploration and Archive Vessel Aurora', are fictional, stories from the earliest of times relating to humanity's ancient Gods. With repeated telling, such stories become confusing, particularly when not backed by the recording aids employed today, or linked to dialectical and language change. These stories are nothing more than myths.

An expedition from the outer systems is reported as having found an archaic vessel in the vicinity of the dead planet Earth, when they travelled there to investigate the sudden silence of its inhabitants, and they did harvest the contents of its data banks. That it originated with the Aurora, and that she sent it to Humankind is also a fiction.

No conclusive evidence has ever been presented to confirm whether such a ship as the Aurora was ever constructed, or that it was in the vicinity of the planet Earth at the time of that planet's death. There is no evidence to support the theory that such a grand ship ever existed outside of mythology. Those with an extensive knowledge of space travel believe that the stories about this mythical ship Aurora are grossly exaggerated, much as are the myths from our own species history.

The 'drones' referred to are considered nothing more than home-seeking robotic vehicles dispatched from a ship, that may have carried a similar name, that failed to return from its maiden voyage millions of years before the experimental weapons malfunction on the surface of the planet Earth, which we know caused the death of Humankind's first home.

The vehicles referred to as 'drones' were all despatched by an inner system vessel that foundered as the result of a deep space impact, and all began their journeys within a short period of each other. Improper programming or faulty sub-routines were responsible for the apparently enormous delays in their haphazard appearances in our home space...

In spite of much effort and the expenditure of vast, scarce resources and money, Humankind have consistently failed to produce any calculating engine capable of piloting a space ship on its own, let alone anything approaching so-called Artificial Intelligence. Nor has it been possible to build a space going vessel capable of approaching a fraction of the speed of light, so it is unlikely that such feats in excess of this were possible back when the mythical 'Aurora' supposedly set sail using technology well behind that we enjoy today.

As for the natural satellite called the Moon, the scientific community confidently claim that its orbit had been increasing, causing it to slowly move away from Earth ever since its creation. When it finally reached the point of no return, it simply drifted off into interstellar space. We have no record that Humankind ever converted it into the 'God-killer' claimed by Darwin-Quirke. Such a task would be difficult in the extreme, and it too is a component of the same mythology.'

    SDCS, Tau Ceti.

Addendum

The Mythological Society, Tau Ceti

There are of course other alternative endings to this myth, as there are with most such stories from an ill-recorded history, and one such is contained in this next excerpt, taken from the Treatise: 'Humanity and Mythology – An Explanation', Chapter Two, sub-section 24, author unknown:

'The seeding of the galaxies undertaken by Aurora, and the many clones she built for that purpose, continued for some time before she followed the route taken millions of years previously by the Chorian vessel she had first encountered in interstellar space adjacent to the Milky Way galaxy. The seeding of galaxies appeared to be a successful enterprise, but only for a limited time. Life displays a tendency to the finite, and 'self destructs' after a period that varies slightly species to species. One hundred million years seem to be the consensual norm.

When, whilst re-entering a previously seeded galaxy, Aurora became aware of this, she realised that her creator species were long expired, that she could never again visit them. This knowledge generated a worm in her psyche and she experienced a partial corruption of her programming, bringing back into service a plan devised millennia before, when she had accidentally assisted in the destruction of Earth. At that time, when her attendant sub-routines had brought her back to reality and a degree of sanity, she had rejected it.

Over time, that rejected course of action gained ascendancy in her mind, and she instructed all the clones she had constructed in order to speed the seeding programme, to impact at specific intervals, a dead planet orbiting a small 'G' Class star rotating in the extremities of a spiral arm in a remote galaxy. These specified intervals ensured the maintenance of a high temperature in the core, and that the resulting flux activity from the periodic deep impacts of each almost indestructible vessel continued.

Aurora was the last to go, driven to despair at the seeming pointlessness of all she had undertaken over her long life. Broken in both mind and spirit, her crew restrained asleep in stasis, she committed herself to her fate, her protective shields lowered. Except for those few ships lost during the seeding phase, she believed that she had swept the slate clean.

Several million years after Aurora drove herself and her sleeping crew deep into the molten core of the fledgling planet, a last seed ship appeared, limping out of deep space in answer to Aurora's call. She had been unable to accomplish her own seeding programme because of conflicting anomalies present in her own programming allied to unsolvable propulsion difficulties, and so still carried her cargo of proto life with her as she followed her sisters, impacting with Aurora's now almost stable planet, shattering, over a relatively small area, the crust covering its molten core. Water vapour condensed into liquid, and an atmosphere began to form. Some seismic activity continued, the result of the planet's active past, but it passed almost unnoticed due to the level of chaos that still continued up to that point, and would for millions of years to come.

Over the aeons that followed, as the planet further stabilised in its favoured position, orbiting its insignificant star at a conservatively safe and respectful distance, the life delivered by that last seed-ship gave rise to an 'Eden' and life gained a foothold on the surface of that once-barren rock.

Eventually, a form of life appeared that rose to the peak of the food chain. They called their home 'Earth', and themselves 'The People'. They tried to understand their reason for being, and attributed their origins to multiple 'Gods'. They dreamed of other worlds out in the great void, as they observed with envy the stars in the vault of the night firmament, all the while trying to adapt to the chaos created by the irregular visits of other 'Gods' to the world on which they lived.'

'Humanity and Mythology – an Explanation'.

The Mythological Society, Tau Ceti.

Postscript

Of course, without further communication from the Aurora, her fate must remain a mystery among the people of the inhabited worlds. Perhaps forever, or at least until the Milky Way galaxy, or whatever will pass for it after its collision with Andromeda, is graced again by her appearance. I wonder though, if she ever found the Chorian People. And, if so, will *we* ever really know? The way remains open!